The Other Side of Desi attitudes toward lesbian than any of Ms. Christia Carrie, has turned her lif bianism, her right to love as she wishes. Eleven years after going "straight," she falls in love with a woman—and hates herself for it. It is a story that is doubtlessly being enacted in towns and cities across America today, where fear of revulsion and ostracism causes women to run from the truth and hide in miserable " security."

Paula Christian's two 1965 novels, Amanda, *and* The Other Side of Desire, *arrived at the end of the now famous Golden Era of Lesbian paperback original novels. Both reflect the changes in editorial policy that had begun to prevail at that time. Thus, they are less sympathetic to Lesbian concerns than their predecessors from Ms. Christian's pen. This does not lessen, however, delightful potential for a new generation of Lesbian readers. In the days of our past when there were few beacons of hope, Paula Christian, together with one or two others, produced books about women we could find appealing, could relate to.* Amanda *and* The Other Side of Desire, *belong in every library of Lesbian literature.*

—Barbara Grier (1981)
The Naiad Press

In this book, Ms. Christian transcends the issue of homosexual or heterosexual love, choosing to deal cleanly and clearly with the all-inclusive issue of human loving.

Carrie doesn't know just what she needs, but what she gets is Kim Willis. What quickly ensues is a lesson in love that perhaps more lesbians have learned than care to admit; the students are the teachers and the grading scale is based not on whom you love, but on how well...."

—Catherine Kemmering

THE OTHER SIDE OF DESIRE

by
Paula Christian

**With a special Foreword
by Joyce Bright**

timely books

p.o. box 267
new milford, connecticut 06776

An original Timely Books edition, published by special
arrangement with the author. First printing March 1981.

Copyright © 1965 by Paula Christian

Library of Congress Card Catalog Number: 81-50051

ISBN 0-931328-08-X

Timely Books
P.O. Box 267
New Milford, CT 06776

THE LESBIAN ROMANCES OF PAULA CHRISTIAN

. . . This is the wonderful stuff of romantic fantasy to which we're all entitled! Paula Christian is the mistress of it, and if you haven't read her, you're missing a treat.

Edge of Twilight was first published in 1959. Twenty-two years later, Timely Books will complete its republication of all six Christian romances. This is an event to be celebrated. After twenty years the demand for her books is greater than ever. The six books together form a kind of lesbian roots, providing a history of the fifties and sixties from a lesbian perspective. More than that, they are fun to read.

The objection to these Christian novels is that they pander to the sensational stereotypes of straight society. Most of the endings have our would-be lesbians returning to the straight life. After all, according to the stereotype, a lesbian's life is immature.

One simply must remember that these books *had* to have those endings. Publishers demanded it. What is so amazing is that some of Christian's characters do get things worked out. Both *Love Is Where You Find It* and *Another Kind of Love* have "happy" endings, holding out the promise of a fulfilling lesbian relationship.

What is disturbing is not that Christian had to incorporate straight stereotypes into her books, but that so many lesbians have in the past, and still today, buy the truth of such stereotyping. So many lesbians who came out in the forties and fifties still carry the psychic damage of that . . . feeling that the lesbian way of life is doomed to be a lonely, unstable, tragic one. Some lesbians still believe that straight is better, and that only a masochist would choose to be gay.

Yes, fulfilling relationships are possible in real life.

Putting aside the stereotyping, there is much that is positive in Christian's novels. Her heroines are really very stable underneath it all. They are productive members of society. These books are not, as the old covers would imply, trashy sex novels. The women, due to Christian's fine writing, are real personalities with occupations. They have dirty dishes in the sink, and serve instant coffee. They also have the courage to face up to their circumstances, and the intelligence to resolve their problems.

Reading between the lines, one discovers the real message in these books, a message to communicate, to love. "How selfish and cruel lovers are . . . to withhold their inner emotions, to dangle their love, doling it out in so many grams per meeting, instead of opening themselves, sharing their love." Let's face it, relationships that last have to be built on more than sexual encounters. Surely lesbians of the future, living in a more open society, can benefit from that wisdom.

But now back to fantasy. During my teens I lived in Ethiopia. There was no television. So we read a great deal, having an abundance of books left behind by departing families. It was in this potpourri of leftover reading material that I discovered *The Well of Loneliness* and, yes, *Edge of Twilight*. Since I came out at the same time, the simultaneous discovery of these books was hugely satisfying.

Thank you Paula Christian.

—*Joyce Bright*

Joyce Bright is swiftly emerging as one of the most perceptive, and best book reviewers of feminist and lesbian-feminist material. Her columns may be read in *Mom . . . Guess What!,* a Sacramento (Calif.) periodical, nationally serving the men and women of the gay community.

Chapter I

Carrie Anderson walked out of the Daitch Shopwell on the Shore Road to her small blue Volkswagen and unloaded her groceries on the back seat. It was a much hotter day than she'd expected, even though it wasn't quite noon; she wished she hadn't worn her light wool plaid skirt. Thinking of that made her remember that she still had to pick up her cleaning and with a tired sigh closed the door of her car, hoped to hell the kid's ice cream wouldn't melt, and started walking down the few doors to the cleaners. It was a funny kind of day, at least to her. Carrie had never been given to moods particularly, in fact, she was really a rather placid type of person; especially since her marriage to Paul. But for some reason during these last days of August with the full trees, the flowers just beginning to fade, she felt restless and even, yes, incomplete in a way.

"Summer fever," she muttered under her breath but secretly wondered if she was going through some kind of early menopause. She had to laugh at that. Barely thirty-five years old and worried about change of life. But the real laugh, the secret she rarely thought about anymore and would certainly never admit, was how ironic it was for her, with her particular past, to be concerned about childbearing. After all, she had Paul Jr. and little Sara, her own favorite, sweet and scrubbed Sara who'd be going into first grade. She sometimes worried about her favoring Sara but not for very long. Paul never noticed it except to tease her because Sara's clothes were the only ones which were really ironed perfectly whether play clothes or dress; and young Paul was too busy with his classmates and homework to notice it. Boys were different anyway. They didn't want their mothers slobbering all over them; they wanted to be men and tough and self-sufficient.

5

Paul Jr. would be quite a guy when he grew up—all right, she thought—and he'd give the girls plenty of trouble with his dark, intense eyes and blond wavy hair. She wondered if he'd keep his nickname, Sambo. Carrie and Paul had started calling him that as soon as he began to walk; he'd learned by pulling himself up holding onto a piece of furniture and would circle an entire room endlessly from one piece to another. She and Paul had laughed a lot in those days watching Sambo make his rounds, but that had been before Paul had opened up his own advertising agency—just about the same time Sara was born—and when they'd had time together in their small place in the Westchester Garden Apartments on Pelham Shore Road in New Rochelle.

Of course, it was tough on Paul commuting into Manhattan to his job but he made a very good—and steady— salary and at least he very rarely had to work late, or take accounts out to dinner and night clubs. When he got home his life was his own. She immediately felt guilty. If there was anything she hated it was one of those whining suburban wives who are so selfish they can't allow their husbands to branch out on their own. They weren't wives; they were parasites. It wasn't because they loved their husbands and wanted to be near them; it was pure boredom because they didn't have enough within themselves to be alone and enjoy it. Well, she wasn't like that and she had no intention of allowing herself to become that way. Paul had started the agency just a little over six and a half years ago and it was just now beginning to pay off, that is, to really pay off so they could think in terms of a nice vacation with the kids. Through careful management, and adhering strictly to their budget, she and Paul had been able to buy an old house when Sara had been about a year old. Nothing fancy, of course, and especially not in New Rochelle where property was so expensive. But it had four bedrooms (one immediately became a den for Paul) and the kids could each have a room to themselves. The furniture was what they laughingly called Early Salvation Army, and the stove and refrigerator were used when they bought

6

them. But with Paul's GI financing benefits, and the cramped but expensive apartment driving them nuts, they'd decided to invest in a house of their own. Carrie had been meaning to speak to Paul about refurnishing it now; little by little of course, but to fix it up. She could still remember how she'd felt that time, several months ago, when she'd asked Paul why he didn't bring his clients to the house once in a while, so he wouldn't have to be out so much and so that she could meet them and take more interest in the agency. All he'd said was, "Here?" It had hurt, more than she wanted to admit, and she never brought it up again. He hadn't meant to be cruel; he was too nice for that. In fact Paul was something of a treasure in a husband. A good provider with initiative, careful in his clothes and manners, soft-spoken, educated (not especially cultured, but educated) and he was never underfoot. He played golf on his days off, took Carrie out to dinner to a nice restaurant twice a month, was good and patient with the children—usually—and thank God! he wasn't a sex fiend. Once a month was the general rule; sometimes several months would go by, and very seldom it might be twice or three times a month.

True, it was her own attitude that had started their sexual patterns. She could still recall their first real argument about it shortly after Sambo had been born. They'd come home from a movie and while Paul drove the sitter home Carrie got ready for bed. She heard his car pull into the driveway while she was brushing her hair, and within minutes he was in the bedroom.

He changed into his pajamas and climbed into bed, sitting up and watching her. "It's funny about men and women," he'd said casually.

"Oh?"

"I mean, like I get a real kick out of watching a woman comb her hair. It's sexually stimulating, y'know. But a woman would never feel that way about a man."

She put the brush down slowly and pretended that his comment was purely an observation and hoped not a build-up. "I guess not," she said, then added, "Think I'll check the baby again."

A few minutes later she returned to the bedroom and got into bed. Paul switched off the lamp and lay still for several moments, then turned and molded his body to fit hers. She could feel him against her and hoped she could feign being almost asleep. His hand slipped through her nightgown and cupped her breast gently. "Turn over, darling," he whispered.

"What?" she murmured.

"C'mon, you're not asleep. Turn over."

"Oh, Paul, not tonight please."

"Why not tonight?" he said. His tone was joking but something in his voice gave away impatience.

"I'm just a little tired, that's all," she answered. "And, well, we just did it the other day. . . ."

Paul sat up in bed abruptly. She could feel him reaching for his cigarettes and saw the reddish glow the match gave the room. "Carrie," he said slowly, "do you have any idea when 'the other day' was?"

She didn't answer him. She didn't really know when they had last made love but it just didn't seem to be so important to her as it was to him. It had been once; before she'd married Paul. It had been even more important to her then—in that other world. But with Paul it was different. He was a good lover, she supposed; he was the only man she'd ever known who could arouse her sexually. Carrie wanted to meet his passion, wanted desperately to do so—but simply couldn't. She wasn't afraid of him, or repulsed either; but she always felt a little ashamed when they made love. It embarrassed her. She knew there was no reason for it—none at all. Yet it did. Maybe she was afraid that that was all he wanted from her, but Carrie basically knew better. She didn't know why she was this way with him, and she knew it hurt him, but there didn't seem to be anything she could do about it.

"Carrie!" Paul's voice sternly demanded. "Let's talk this out, shall we? I'm sorry if I sound like I'm giving you hell," he said more gently, "but that's what you've been

8

putting me through. I've got to get this settled and it may as well be now. Are you listening?"

"Yes, Paul," she said but couldn't help wishing she were three thousand miles away.

"We made love exactly three weeks ago! Three *weeks!* Don't you think that's unfair to me? I love you, Carrie, deeply. But I can't live on sex once a month. I'm not just a man, I'm a human being. What's the matter with you? Do you think it's just lust on my part?"

"No, Paul." She could feel the tears of guilt in her eyes but had nothing to say. What could she tell him when she didn't know herself.

"Sex is just another way of showing my love for you, a way of holding us together even more closely. It isn't just for making babies, it's a pleasure two people in love share . . . except you and me. I can't take much more of this, Carrie," he said softly.

She rolled over and buried her face in his chest. "I just don't understand, Paul . . . really. Why does it *have* to be three-point-one times per week . . . or *any* set number of times. Shouldn't it be when both of us want to?"

"Sure," Paul answered slowly, "but you never do." He placed his hand on her head and touched her face. "I've tried to be patient and understanding, Carrie. I kept hoping that if I didn't force the issue you'd come around on your own. But all you ever did was either pull away or make a joke of it. Are you afraid to love? And then I thought if I were more agressive you might respond and I began demanding it of you. But I couldn't keep it up; I don't want to force anyone to do something as intimate as that against her will. And then I decided to let you go as long as you wanted without it . . . I don't suppose you remember that. It was three months before I broke down and touched you again."

She didn't remember it at all, but didn't dare admit it.

"Carrie, you make me feel dirty, and that's wrong. My needs are natural and your aversion is not." He paused and Carrie could feel his body tense with emotion. "Carrie . . . I never asked you about your past and I don't really want to know now. Just one thing and that's all."

She closed her eyes tightly; panic and fear roaring through her body.

"Did you marry me on the rebound? Had there been someone else?"

Carrie wished she could die. There was nothing she dared tell him—not without losing the marriage. Wasn't it perhaps better to let him think there had been another man? Wasn't it kinder than what she would otherwise expose him to? She didn't know, would perhaps never know, but there wasn't time to think of some carefully fabricated story to appease him and in desperation she forced herself to nod. She wanted to cry and scream out the truth but knew she couldn't.

"I had thought as much," he whispered. "Did you have this same aversion to sex then? I'm not going to be jealous, Carrie, I just have to know where I stand."

"No." Her voice was barely audible.

"But you do love me? Oh, not in the same way, of course, I know better than that. But love and respect?"

She put her arms around him and clung to him. "Oh, yes, Paul. I do love you . . . I don't know what's wrong with me . . . it's not your fault . . . but then I don't see why it has to be anyone's fault. I just don't think it's as important as you do, I guess."

He snorted. It's taken me a long time, but I agree with you. It's not my fault; I know that now. And, I guess, it's not really yours either. . . ."

"What are you going to do now?" she asked, afraid, and really not wanting to know.

"I haven't decided, Carrie. Something. I can't keep this up. You don't want to make love as often as I need to and there's nothing I can do to change that evidently. I love you too, darling, but our situation just isn't fair."

"Oh, Paul! Is sex so damn important? Isn't love enough? Our home, our son, each other? Why should it outweigh everything else we have . . . endanger our marriage?"

"I hate to sound pedantic, Carrie, but I'm afraid if you

10

haven't got it you'll never understand. It isn't going to break up our marriage, at least, not if I can help it. But I cannot live this way!"

"That's the same as admitting you want a divorce," Carrie said. "Is that what you want?" She was terrified he'd say yes; but somewhere inside she almost hoped he would. She'd wanted children, and now she had Paul Jr. She did love Paul, but he forced her to live in constant fear and guilt, constant anxiety.

"No. I told you, darling, I *do* love you. All it means is that I'll probably have to look elsewhere for what I can't get at home."

"That's a horrible thing to say!" she nearly yelled and sat up in anger. "Then sex is all that matters to you . . . you'd go to bed with anybody just for a dirty roll in the hay?"

"You just don't understand, Carrie," he said slowly, his face contorting with frustration. "I don't want to go elsewhere—but what choice are you giving me!"

"I'd leave you, Paul. I swear it!" Carrie burst out into tears and turned her back on him.

He let her cry then said, "Then it's you who is ruining the home because of sex, Carrie, not me. You won't provide it for me. . . ."

"I do too!"

"Once a month is not a lovelife!"

She laid on her side staring into the dark. She saw him light another cigarette and wished she were dead. She knew there was nothing she could do about it, about Paul's needs or her own reactions. "If I ever find out about it I'll leave you, Paul."

"Is that some kind of left-handed permission?" he asked sarcastically.

"I don't see that I have much to say about it."

"You could tell me what bothers you, how we could solve this problem. It's inside you, not me."

She wasn't too sure what she'd answered him then. It was so long ago. Ten years, she thought, and wondered if Paul had really gone through with his threat of outside

11

satisfaction. Nothing between them had changed; at least on the surface. He never brought up the subject again and she was grateful for that—and too frightened to ever question him or try to find out, in any way, if he was going elsewhere. She did try to be more responsive after that argument, never put him off regardless of what she would have preferred. What did it matter, she reasoned, since she would always prefer that he left her alone. But he kept his demands to a minimum, or perhaps he'd accustomed himself to not needing sex so much. Whatever he was doing, or however he'd resolved it, she would never ask. It was a good marriage, she was sure of that; and eleven years was a long time.

Carrie returned to the car with her cleaning and hung up Paul's suit by the rear window, lowered herself into the driver's seat, bumped her shin and thought son-of-a-bitch but said damn, and closed the door. Seconds later she was pulling into their driveway, just off Centre Avenue near New Rochelle College. She didn't like being so near a Catholic girls' school; it reminded her too much of things she'd rather forget; but it was a minor inconvenience only. As she shut off the engine, she could see Sara coming home from a neighbor's and automatically knew what Sara's first words would be.

"Ice cream, Mommie? Ice cream?" Sara always spoke in half-sentences. She knew better, but conserved herself for some private reason.

Carrie smiled at the familiar little voice and its plaintive tone; the big round gray eyes staring in earth-shaking suspense. "Yes, Sara. I got ice cream. Two kinds today, darling."

"Banilla?" Sara took a small sack of vegetables from the large box on the back seat and helped carry in the groceries. "Banilla?"

"V-anilla, darling, and peach for Sambo. Have a nice time next door?" Carrie was careful not to let the back door slam so she could bawl the kids out if they did it.

"No. I'm not playing with Birginia anymore. She's mean."

12

"Why's V-irginia mean? Did you do something wrong?" It took great effort to admit Sara could do anything wrong, but Carrie didn't want to raise a houseful of brats so she always thought it best to keep an open mind.

"I hit her," Sara said and smiled smugly.

Carrie could hardly keep from laughing. "Well, wouldn't you be mean if she hit you?"

"She did . . . first. I wanted to play with her doll and she wouldn't let me so I told her mommie and when I came back Birginia hit me. So I hit her. And then her mommie said we had to be nice or we couldn't play anymore so we didn't play. And I'm never never going to play with her anymore."

"Did you ask her nicely to play with her doll?" Carrie put away the last of the groceries and began to wash the fruit and vegetables.

"I said please."

"Tell me exactly how you asked," Carrie prompted.

"I said, 'Please let me play with your doll, Birginia,' just like that." Sara posed as she said it, with her arms straight down at her sides and standing erect like she would for Show-and-Tell in school.

"Are you sure?" she asked. Somehow Carrie found it difficult to believe that Sara had been so formal with a playmate.

Sara nodded violently with that wonderful childilke belief that energy confirms truth, and a frown is a sworn oath. "Well," Carrie said finally, "maybe it was her favorite doll and she was afraid you'd hurt it or something. She must've had a good reason. Virginia's a nice little girl and she wouldn't say no unless she had a reason. She lets you play with her other toys, doesn't she? And you have a few toys you won't let her play with either."

"She didn't have to hit me," Sara reasoned firmly.

"You didn't have to be a tattletale either." The back door slammed and Carrie instinctively yelled out, "Sambo!"

"Aw, Mom."

"Go on. . . ."

Paul Jr. returned to the back stairs and reentered the

13

house without slamming the door. "Couldn't Dad fix it instead like some people have with those things that don't let the door slam?"

"Your father works very hard and very late just to keep you clothed and fed. I should think it wouldn't be asking too much of you to be considerate enough to let him enjoy what little time he has to relax. You've got hands and you've got muscles and somewhere inside that head there has to be brains—use them and the door won't slam, you won't have to go outside and do it over again, I'll be happy, and your father can rest."

"Brother!" Sambo muttered throwing his baseball into the air and catching it. "When's lunch? Me and the guys are gonna play some ball afterwards and they're already eating."

"The boys and I," Carrie corrected, "and lunch's going to be ready in about fifteen minutes. If you're in a hurry fix yourself a sandwich—not jelly."

"I'm not a girl," he said churlishly.

"Neither is the chef at the Ritz. Put up or shut up, son."

"Oh, all right. What can I have?" Sambo opened up the refrigerator and pulled out the bread and some mayonnaise. "Have we got any bologna?"

"You're standing there," Carrie laughed. "You tell me."

"Guess you're right," he grinned back and as would be expected pulled out the lunchmeat from directly in front of him, then made his sandwich—not without little kicking gestures at Sara who was now standing at his elbow. She remained unperturbed. "Hey, Mom," Sambo said in his slow way that meant he wanted something.

"Um-hm."

"When school starts next month and now that I'm ten years old, couldn't I please join the Scouts? All the gang belong 'cept Gus and he's too fat anyway."

"That's not nice to say about Gus, and there's plenty of time to think about joining the Scouts."

"But all the other guys have belonged for *years!* They know a lotta things I don't an' it kinda makes me look

14

goofy," Sambo said and took an enormous bite of sandwich.

"Put those things back, please."

"Okay, but what about the Scouts, Mom. Dad said he was a Scout when he was a kid."

Carrie tossed him an apple from off the sideboard and said, "We've plenty of time, Sambo. I'll ask your father about it."

"He doesn't care . . ."

"Sambo . . ."

"All right. Can I go now?" His sandwich had disappeared.

"Soon as you put away your lunch things." She watched him stuff the bread and mayonnaise back into the refrigerator in any random place, wave his hand and run through the back door. She waited for it to slam but it never came. He must really want to join the Scouts, she thought, and wondered what she was going to do about it. She'd put it off for so many years now, always with the same excuse to Paul who didn't really understand her reluctance; that Sambo was too young to take care of himself if anything happened like a bus accident or during a field trip. She hadn't dared tell Paul the real reason, that she'd known a homosexual once who'd been introduced to it by one of those auxiliary leaders. Maybe it had been a fluke, and then maybe it hadn't been. But she didn't want the same thing to happen to Sambo. She didn't want either of her children to ever hear the word much less be associated in any way with homosexuals. And there was no reason why they should if she raised them right, any more than they would ever have to know about criminals or dope addicts or drunks. It would never be a part of their world, that's all. She didn't have this attitude from any kind of moral judgment, per se; it came from something entirely different. But this year, well, perhaps Sambo was old enough now to take care of himself—in all ways. He was a husky boy and all-male; not an ounce of anything effeminate about him . . . thank God. And if anyone tried any hanky-panky with him now, well, he was old enough to fight or yell for

15

help; he was old enough to know what was right and what was wrong.

Ten years, she thought, and for the first time in those years she felt herself getting old. Not really old, of course, but that awful knowledge that youth is gone and all she had to look forward to was watching her children grow up, and grandchildren. She desperately hoped Paul's business would settle down to a quiet rat race in a few years so she might enjoy some companionship again. There didn't seem to be very much for them to say to each other anymore. Business, of course, to some degree, and the latest antics of the kids, but nothing genuinely between them as adults; no mutual outside interests—Paul didn't have time or new topics to throw around and discuss the way they used to when they were first married. She supposed in a way that that was natural, that all married couples went through that stage while the kids were growing up and husbands had to work so hard to get established. And Carrie took a great deal of pride in knowing that Paul was in business for himself, and a highly competitive business at that. There certainly weren't many men left in the world who had the guts to take a chance, not when they had families to support. But even so, there didn't seem to be very much for her to occupy her time with, much less her mind. Oh, she'd have lunch or coffee with "Birginia's" mother, Elaine Henderson, every once in a while, but for the most part Carrie wasn't too outgoing in the sense of enjoying the popular suburban sport of coffee klatches. She wasn't the type of mother who felt it necessary to give detailed descriptions of her children's bowel movements to all the neighbors, much less compare the price of laundry soap. And she resented television unless there was a special play or something. She read all the best-sellers, but even they didn't seem to be very inspiring. A couple of times she'd tried to read informative non-fiction but she'd found it difficult to concentrate on them. Carrie joined the PTA every year but never attended the meetings; she'd gone once and it had filled her with utter horror, and it was the only time she felt she might become an alcoholic

16

. . . had there been anything present to ease her into the habit.

She suddenly became aware of Sara sitting on the floor peering up under her skirt and laughed. She leaned over and picked her up. "Hey, fatso, you're getting too heavy."

"Ice cream?"

"Lunch first. How about a nice hamburger with a bun, hmm?"

Sara put her arms around Carrie's neck and hugged hard. "I love you, Mommie," she said and then wriggled to get down.

"I love you too," she answered and let Sara slide out of her arms slowly. She took a pattie out of the freezer and put it on to fry.

Later on in the day, while Sara was taking her afternoon nap and Sambo was out Lord-knows-where playing ball, Carrie went into her bedroom and sat in front of the mirror looking at herself. Ten years, she kept thinking and tried to remember how she'd looked when her light brown hair had been cut close to her head instead of in the Lauren Bacall style she wore now; it was pretty hair and she knew it. Thick and heavy with enough blond in it to catch the light and glisten. Her face was about the same, though, still the straight eyebrows and the large, clear hazel eyes that deceitfully gave the appearance of never having had an evil thought behind them, and her face still had the strong bones and hollow cheeks so popular these days. She had never been a pretty girl, in the traditional sense, but always very attractive—even in a boy's shirt and slacks. Her figure had filled out some since those days, especially her hips and her breasts. Not fat, but more rounded, more womanly. Well, ten years and two kids can do that to you, she decided. And then, without any logical reason, she also decided that she would get a job once school started. A part-time job, of course, since she didn't want to deprive the children of her attention, but something where she could get out and meet people. Something to do with her time and to talk to Paul about. She didn't think he'd mind; he wasn't a stuffed shirt about those

17

things, and anyway it would be rather nice to have a little pin money for herself; maybe treat herself to the beauty parlor regularly or if she was lucky enough to find something that paid a little more, to even put aside for an extra nice vacation to Europe in a few years. Something she and Paul could share and enjoy; she was sure Paul's mother would take the kids for a month or so.

Suddenly she felt very excited, and very pleased with herself. She hoped Paul would be able to get home early tonight so she could talk to him about it—maybe he could make some suggestions about what type of work she should look for (she'd never been an especially good stenographer but her typing used to be quite fast). She went into the bathroom to take her afternoon shower and get ready for Paul to come home and found herself whistling—just a little sharp of the key—"I've Been Workin' On The Railroad. . . ."

Chapter II

After her conversation with Paul that night, and her solemn word that a job would never interfere with her duties as a wife and a mother, Carrie began to read the Help Wanted —Female section of the *Standard Star* nightly. It wasn't too encouraging, even as Paul had predicted, mostly for household help, file clerks full time, or genius girl-Fridays at half the salary they might get in Manhattan. The paper itself would occasionally advertise for girls to take ads over the phone, but it was full time. She had not thought to look so soon for work, after all there was a month yet before she could begin; but Paul had assured her it would not be easy and she should start right away if she wanted to find anything before all the other housewives started looking too. He'd been very sweet about the idea, though. Even a little paternal despite how tired he was after working until a bit past ten.

"Well, honey, if you think you'd like to, why go ahead. But you know, working takes a lot out of a person, even easy work. How're you going to manage the house and the errands and everything?" He stood up from the dining-room table and walked into the living room, slowly and with ease as he did everything, and lowered himself into the old overstuffed chair that was doubtlessly the ugliest piece of furniture in existence—and the most comfortable.

She followed him and stood next to the large window facing the street, conscious of posing a little like the youngest son going out to save the family name. "That's the whole point, Paul," she tried to keep the excitement out of her voice. "I thought maybe something that would only require two or three days a week, something where the hours would be flexible."

Paul snorted. "Sure. Like what?"

"That's why I need your advice . . . I don't know."

"Now look, honey. I can understand your wanting to get away from the house and kids for awhile, and the idea of having your own personal money must have its attraction, but I'm afraid you don't know what you're up against. Business has changed a lot in the last ten years. If they want someone part time they get a kid out of school, so they don't waste their time training someone who couldn't possibly make a career of it. What do you suppose your typing speed is by now? You haven't even seen a typewriter since we were married."

"Well, that's another thing I'd like to get with the extra money," Carrie said defensively. "It'd be nice for Sambo when he has to start term papers and things."

"What! Five, six years from now? C'mon, honey, be reasonable. You want to get out. Fine. I can understand that," he said gently with his serious, dark look that Sambo had inherited. "But the agency is picking up and I'll be able to get all these things when the time comes. You're just rationalizing about the money, now aren't you."

Carrie felt thwarted and terribly foolish. The money angle had been her biggest argument and it vanished now like so many particles of deodorant spray. "I suppose so,

Paul, but it doesn't seem like it to me." The last was to save face.

He gave a priestly nod while fishing out a cigarette, then fumbled in his pants pockets for matches—something he seemed to be doing eternally. Carrie thought she'd like to buy him a lighter for his birthday, not so much to make him happy as to rid herself of his fumblings. He found some finally and lighted his cigarette with his little ritual— read the cover of the matchbook first, slowly bend one match, contemplate it as if it were an engineering feat to remove it, tear it off, hold it a second suspended over the book, strike it and raise it to his cigarette, bring it slowly to the tip, inhale once vigorously while holding the burning match to one side, watch the end smoke and ashen for a moment. Then a quiet sigh, a vigorous flick of the wrist to extinguish the match and a careless tossing it aside like a used up condom. It never varied. Finally he'd look at Carrie across the room with time-ripened appreciation but just a hint of being put upon at that particular moment. Carrie didn't resent his attitude; she didn't even really notice it that much since her own father had been very much like Paul and she was more than used to it.

"Have you thought about going to school instead?" Paul asked her.

"Of course I have," she lied quickly and surprised herself in the doing; it was exactly the kind of lie she used to tell her parents all the time so they wouldn't patronize her. But Paul wasn't her father or her mother and she didn't see why she should have to react that way to him. "That is, I *thought* of it but really, Paul, there's nothing I really want to study and no matter what you say, I really am looking forward to a little money of my own. Just to throw it away if I want to," she knew she shouldn't have said that but it was too late. "Of course, that's an extreme example. . . ."

"I'll say it is!" he answered and, to her relief, laughed. "Tell you what, hon."

"What," she tried to be casual but knew him well enough to realize there was a bargain in it somewhere.

"You go ahead and look around. Who knows, you might

20

be lucky," he smiled with an expression of no-offense-but-really-what-do-you-have-to-offer, "and if you don't find anything by the time the kids are back in school for a month—that gives you two months, or so—you'll agree to forget about it for this year. How's that?"

She didn't really doubt that she could find something within two months, but she didn't like the "forget about it" clause in case she hadn't. "That seems fair. . . ."

"One hitch, though."

Here it comes, she thought. "I'm not to apply at your office?" He liked little jokes.

"Say, that would be funny wouldn't it? But, seriously, my only restriction is that I don't want you waiting on people. Not in a restaurant, or department store, or any-place else connected with the general public. It wouldn't look good for business. That's not asking too much, is it?"

"No," she said with complete honesty. "I don't think I'd want to anyway, but I can certainly understand your viewpoint." It struck her then how much they talked alike, the same vocabulary, almost the same inflections. There wasn't anything new or stimulating about them at all, nothing at all, and it had never been so glaringly apparent as it was right then. Carrie suddenly felt very sorry for them both, compassionate as only a woman can be who believes she alone can see a situation clearly. She crossed over to his chair and, leaning over, kissed him lightly on the forehead. "Thank you, Paul. You're always so con-siderate."

"And you're always smart enough to tell me," he said and smiled. "You might have the right idea, Carrie . . . it was kind of fun having something to discuss and decide tonight, sort of took my mind off business and relaxed me. And if you went to school I might get jealous of your knowing more than I do."

Carrie straightened up and felt very close to Paul, more than she had in a long time. Close, and almost grateful. "Bad day today?" she asked after a moment.

"Not too. Got a new account . . . concrete manufac-turer."

"Did he give you a contract?"

"No, not yet. Sort of on spec. But it could be a big one if I bring it off right. Mostly trade magazine copy, but I think I'll try to talk them into some billboards in the industrial sections around the country. Something catchy."

Carrie giggled.

"What's funny?" he asked.

"I was just thinking you could use a slogan like that book title, you know the one, *Christ In Concrete.*"

"It'd go over big in Rio de Janeiro. . . ."

They laughed and there was a bit of the old days in it. "You're in good shape tonight," Paul said.

"Yep. Think I'll celebrate my coming career with a go at the dishes."

"Well, I'm going to run upstairs and take a fast shower, then read a while in bed. Haven't done that in ages."

"That's right," Carrie said entering the dining room to clear off his dinner dishes, "you haven't."

She'd cleaned up the few things and gone upstairs to the bedroom where Paul was lying comfortably in the big double bed reading *Ad Age.* He turned off the light almost immediately after she got into bed, and she heard the pages fall to the floor. She felt a little silly as the thought entered her head that this would be twice this month and business was good; but on the other hand, she was glad he wanted to—it made the evening sort of a celebration, topped it off.

* * * *

Three days later Carrie went on her first interview and she hadn't been so nervous since her first date with Paul— which came after several years of not dating men at all. She fretted about her make-up, worried that she might look like some old dowager trying to look younger, and more worried that with very little make-up she was still young enough to look like a Beatnik of sorts. In utter frustration she finally decided to use the same make-up she'd use to go to the market; enough to give her a little color and point out her better features, but not so much as to convey an arduous toilet. Fortunately, her complexion was healthy and good; it wasn't olive, or sallow, or milk white or anything else outstanding, just plain clear womanly skin and it didn't require anything special to make it look young and wholesome. She put on her black summer suit, looked at herself in the mirror, approved, thought to put just a dash more of perfume between her breasts then decided against it, glanced again at the address in Larchmont, and torn between hesitating and running went down the stairs to the car with thirty-five minutes to spare before her appointment—in case she had a flat tire or something.

All the way up the Post Road she kept turning over in her mind the lead line of the ad: HOUSEWIVES—BE YOUR OWN BOSS! An advertising research firm needed interviewers—she could only guess what that might involve—and the work could be done on her own schedule; they didn't care how or when as long as you got it back to them in time. There'd been no mention of salary or any special skills required other than liking to meet people. But she'd find out about all that shortly. ARMBREWSTER RESEARCHERS, INC. It did have a strong, professional sound to it all right.

"And what does your husband do," Mrs. Rockefeller would say.

"Oh, he's in advertising too. His own agency, y'know."

"And doesn't he object to your career?"

"Well, he did at first,"—a between-us-girls smile—"but of course, that didn't last long. . . ."

A honking Buick convertible passing and cutting in front of Carrie at the Larchmont Avenue intersection brought her mind back to a more practical line of thinking and she began to watch the cross streets to find the address. She spotted a corner building about a block up that looked like it might be it—it was new, and she wanted everything to be new today. She just had to get the job and

23

that was all there was to it; and she would be good at it, no question about it.

*   *   *   *

"Mrs. Anderson?" the secretary said in the doorway leading to the personnel manager's office as a rather plump, friendly looking applicant came out.

Carrie jumped at the sound of her name and hoped no one had noticed. "Yes, yes . . . I'm Mrs. Anderson."

"You're next, dear," the secretary said and smiled benignly.

Carrie hated to be called "dear" and particularly by strangers but tried not to let her irritation show as she followed the woman into the manager's office. She'd barely gotten through the door when the secretary pulled it closed as she left. Carrie couldn't help feeling somewhat like Jane Eyre as her eyes took in the small, bare room painted that horrible depressing beige color so many offices use. There was only one picture on the wall, a black and white photograph of Cape Cod; one window with flowered paper curtains; one file cabinet with the third drawer hanging open; one desk, and behind it one man—a very tired looking man somewhere in his fifties with the puffy redness of someone who drinks more than his complexion can handle. There was a straight wooden chair next to the desk and Carrie wasn't sure whether she should just go ahead and sit down or wait to be asked; she decided on the first, reasoning that an interviewer should be a little more aggressive than just a secretary or office clerk.

The manager hadn't looked up yet. "Harumph, ahem, gylmp. Your name, please?"

His voice made her think of the Mojave. "Carrie Anderson."

"Mrs.? Miss? Harumph, ahem, gylmp."

"Mrs." she answered quickly. "My husband's name is Paul."

He rifled through several applications and pulled out one; she could tell it was hers from her broad-stroked handwriting. "Harumph, Paul Anderson, ahem, gylmp, Paul Anderson . . . doesn't he have an agency . . . oh yes! You've written it down here." He looked up then and scrutinized her with faded, watery blue eyes. "Business not so good, eh?" He gave a wheezing short laugh to indicate he was joking.

"Business," Carrie smiled back, "is very good, but the children will be in school soon and I wanted something to occupy my time." She caught his glance over her crossed legs and uncrossed them very slowly and very deliberately. It was at times like that she remembered how much she hated most men, the lecherous, one-track, grabby-fingered studs—and also how very lucky she was to have someone like Paul.

"Then, harumph, you should certainly know a little bit about the advertising business, eh? A little bit about what makes this great country of ours the leading nation in the world. Eh? Right?"

She couldn't quite see the correlation between the two but let it go. "Well, just a little about my husband's kind of advertising. I'm not sure that ARMBREWSTER caters to the same kind of accounts. . . ."

"At least you know that there are different kinds of advertising." He grinned at her as if she just come out best in a Regency test. "That's a good start, yes, a very good start." He leaned back expansively and cleared his throat some more. "We like to see new agencies come along, Mrs. Anderson, like it very much. Means more business for us eventually, eh?" Another wheezing laugh came out of his mouth. "Now then, you know about television ratings, don't you, of course you do. Well, we do pretty much the same. Company comes to us and wants to know what little ol' John Q. Public thinks of his product, why he buys it or doesn't buy it, food, television sets, clothing, just about every kind of product there is—long as it's legit, if you get my point."

Carrie nodded and wondered how anyone so obnoxious could ever have become a personnel manager. He was more the type of person who'd make a living selling elixers to a leper colony, and she shuddered slightly at her own imagery.

"So we get our best brains together and devise a questionnaire to suit the product. Sometimes a company just wants to find out how they can improve their advertising copy or slogans, or if they should change the label on a can . . . whatever it is, we find out for them. We always find out, harumph, ahem, gylmp, and that's where the interviewers come in, eh? You go out to people's homes, to the heart of this great country, walk right into their living rooms, their kitchens, and talk to the people, get the pulse of America so to speak. We've got interviewers all over the country and if the product is a nationally distributed one, why, we get a cross-section poll. . . ."

"This," Carrie interrupted softly, "hasn't anything to do with standing in markets and handing out samples and things," she asked remembering Paul's "hitch."

"Of course not!" he answered with as much vehemence as a husband protecting his wife's reputation. "This is advertising, not peddling. Our interviewers are proud of their work, proud of their part in forming the opinions of this nation of ours."

Oh my God! Carrie thought and wished she hadn't asked. For once in her life she wished she could produce a Communist membership card instead of a social security card; it would be worth anything to see his 50-star-studded face. Was this an interview or a rally? "I just wanted to be certain," she added with a comradely smile.

"And that's precisely the kind of attitude ARMBREWSTER is looking for, someone who isn't afraid to ask questions, to check and doublecheck that there's no misunderstanding. You can easily imagine what would happen if an interviewer were sloppy, Mrs. Anderson, wrote down the wrong information or for lack of checking through gave the wrong impression of the right information."

Carrie wondered briefly if she'd have to pass a Security check to be hired. "Your ad didn't mention salary, Mr. . . ." she paused significantly.

"Arnold, Arnold's the name," he said and puffed a little.

Wouldn't you know it, she thought. "Is the salary about the same as regular office work? Or do you pay more because of the importance of personality and thoroughness. . . ."

His mouth slackened somewhat before screwing up for a new delivery. "We think we pay rather well, especially when you consider that your hours are your own and that you have no direct daily supervision. Of course, you get paid by the job, harumph, we couldn't afford to pay you in between jobs when you're not doing anything, could we?" Wheeze-laugh.

"You mean the work isn't steady?" She hadn't expected that.

"Why, no, it isn't. When the company gets an assignment that requires field research then our interviewers get an assignment. Many of our accounts don't require interviewers; sometimes it's a simple—relatively, of course—matter of gathering data on competitive products, their advertising, what market they appeal to, and so on. That sort of thing we can do right here with our regular staff."

"I see," she said. It came as a bitter blow to her high expectations, however vague they had been. But as Mr. Arnold continued with his advertising pledge of allegiance and explained the duties more fully, if not dramatically, she decided that she was in no position to quibble about anything. It would be a start, and probably amusing to "get the pulse of America", and the freedom of hours would leave her time to continue to look for a more dependable job if she wanted to. She didn't doubt for a moment that she was hired; she'd already been in his office twice as long as the woman before her. And she was already taking a certain pride in herself, in a new confidence she was gaining. It was as if there were two Carrie Andersons, wife and mother, of course, but also an independent and capable woman. Suddenly her mind flashed back for a split-second to eleven years before and she quickly put out of her mind that there certainly were two Carrie Andersons, and one of them she never wanted to see or think about again.

She spent about another five minutes in the verbal clutches of ARMBREWSTER's personnel manager and returned home with a pamphlet on advertising research, sample questionnaires, and Mr. Arnold's parched personal American guarantee that she'd be called in for a briefing within a week or two, not to worry.

The first thing she did as she entered the door was to call Elaine Henderson to tell her she could send Sara home now if she wanted to. She spent a few minutes on the phone telling her about the interview to which Elaine cryptically summarized, "I think you're nuts. You couldn't get me to go back to work for anything." But Carrie didn't let that bother her. She knew Elaine's attitude was like so many wives around suburbia, that the sole purpose of a husband is to be relieved of ever having to put on a girdle at seven in the morning. Carrie made herself a cup of coffee and drank it before going into the shower to see if Sara came right home or not. Since she didn't Carrie assumed that she and "Birginia" had made up, or more than likely not even remembered their disagreement a few days before. Finally she put her dirty cup in the sink and with an unusual sense of triumph left it there unwashed.

"I've got more *important* things to do," she said aloud and surveyed the kitchen with a look of disdainful supremacy.

Chapter III

Paul stood before the open suitcase on the bed holding a broad-striped necktie in one hand and a narrow-striped one in the other. "What do you think, hon? After all, it's Chicago not Indianapolis."

Carrie turned from the mirror on her dressing table and gazed at the two ties carefully; her taste in men's clothes was exceptional and Paul always valued her opinion, had even complimented her numerous times for being one of the few women who understood how a man felt about his clothes, his appearance.

"This one brings out the color of my eyes better," he said.

She laughed. "Brown eyes don't have a color that comes out."

"Of course they do. Fat lot you know about it."

"I don't know, Paul. I like the other one better."

"That's because you bought it. Okay. In it goes and out you go, matey." Ever since his hitch in the Navy he'd used the jargon whenever possible, and Carrie was always amazed at how many times that was. Fortunately, by the time Carrie had met him Paul had already returned from Korea and had been discharged. Even though Paul had never been the kind of guy who always talked about his war experiences, he did—especially at that time—often make fun of "the Navy way" and particularly at their dedication to wasting ability; they'd somehow channeled Paul into being a machinist's mate. One of Paul's few friends, and one he'd met during the service, had a Ph.D. in music, yet he had been ship's cook.

"Do you think you'll be gone more than three days?" she asked.

"Doubt it. I can't think of anything that would louse up the contract. In fact, I might even get back sooner." He walked around the bed and put his hands on Carrie's shoulders. "Thursday for sure, but being as I'm so smart maybe sooner. Miss me?"

She looked at him through the mirror. "Of course."

"New job hasn't introduced you to any handsome young men begging for your attention?"

She shook her head. "All I meet is bored housewives and a lot of kids running in and out the door. It's really amazing how some women don't even try to discipline their kids, you know that Paul?"

"I guess. Never thought too much about it since Sambo

and Sara are pretty regular guys. Never any real trouble with them."

"You'd think for their own peace and quiet mothers would want to teach their kids some manners."

"Speaking of Sambo," Paul said holding on to a length of hair around Carrie's neck, "seems it's Scout time again. Says you were going to check with me about it."

Carrie put her brush down very slowly. "It's so late, Paul, and you have to get up so early for your flight. Couldn't we talk about it when you get back?" She hoped he'd let it drop but knew he wouldn't, and also knew that this time she'd have to give in. Since she'd started the job things had been almost better than ever between them; they laughed more and talked more and Paul went out of his way to take an interest in her assignments. She knew that part of it was just professional interest, but still he didn't have to—it was more plain considerateness than anything else. And it wasn't as if they had more time than before. Paul still worked just as hard and just as long, but at least when he did come home there was something new happening and she always had one or two funny incidents to tell him about. And she was so much happier these days, more patient with the children—especially after seeing other people's brats—and less resentful of the time Paul spent at the office or on business trips like the one tomorrow. And it had its effect on Paul too. He was more outgoing with her, more confiding about details and the portent of a client's raised eyebrow; as if her being in the business world gave her a special understanding she had not had before, a kinship of interest. It had brought about many subtle changes in their relationship, even in such a short while. She could sense that he felt less like just the provider, the man who does all the dirty work and everyone takes for granted, not that he'd ever have allowed himself to be conscious of such an outlook or even that Carrie would ever really think of him that way. But Carrie had first-hand knowledge of what it was to have unsuspected feelings, and she was a near expert on controlling them so that they stayed out of her mind; at least, while she was

30

awake. No. Not to give in about the Scouts now would be stupid and cruel. Not because of Sambo, particularly, but just because of the new closeness between herself and Paul. It would soil a part of it, destroy it even, and she herself had already secretly admitted long ago that she was being foolish about the whole matter. She also sensed that it would be unwise to let Paul take this trip without settling it.

Carrie stood up and began to turn the bed down as he moved the two-suiter over to a chair. "I guess I've just been silly," she said lightly.

"What's that?" He turned and looked at her as if he didn't have the foggiest notion of what she was talking about.

"About Sambo's joining the Scouts," she said mildly annoyed since this was her moment of grand concession.

"I don't get you, honey," he said. He put on a fresh pair of pajamas. "Hey, how about this button? This's the second time now. . . ."

She ignored his complaint. "What I'm trying to tell you, Commander, is that I'm agreeing with you. I guess Sambo can take care of himself all right now."

"Say, that's swell, hon. He'll be awfully pleased about that. Did you pack my black socks?"

Carrie barely managed to get out a grunted yes. For three years they'd been discussing the only child-rearing disagreement they'd ever had in their entire married lives and there he was, half asleep, and thinking about his socks. Men! she thought ruthlessly and immediately realized it wasn't a very safe thought and put it away. She put out the light and climbed between the cool sheets, pulling the blanket up around her bare shoulders.

"That's my job," Paul said softly and tucked her gently into his arms. Seconds later he was breathing heavily and she hated herself for having been cross with him, even if he hadn't known she was.

*   *   *   *

Carrie had already been to see three housewives by ten-

31

thirty the next morning. The kids had taken their lunch to school for a change so she wouldn't have to worry about the time it would take to drive home, make lunch, see them back to school, and drive somewhere to resume interviewing. She wanted to wind up this assignment; she was tired of it. Vitamins! Who cared about vitamins? Just for a change, she left the Mamaroneck area and drove back toward her old neighborhood in New Rochelle where she and Paul had first been married. Maybe it was a means of seeking solace while he was away, but she doubted it. It wasn't that she didn't love him, but she was always sort of glad when he was on a business trip. She couldn't have articulated why, but she resented his staying late at the office much more. It was something like going on a diet or not having anything to eat anyhow. She drove past the new school, Trinity, over Church Street and the new extension of the street across the pond—well, new to her, anyway—and toward the new houses recently erected. She didn't like the homes; not at all. They were tasteless constructions of prefabricated mediocrity to her. Costly tributes to mass production and alarming conformity. Her own home, she knew, had probably been just as ugly in its day but at least its day was over and one could now view it as a whimsical proof of yesteryear's poor taste; its age lent it a certain dignity. The houses on the right-hand side of the street were more like her own and, with the power of priority, had a kind of withdrawal from the nouveau riche homes across the street; perhaps it was that the trees were aged and the lawns settled. Carrie pulled the Volkswagen up to one side of the street and parked with a determined sigh. There were at least forty houses along that area and if every other person were at home and would give her time for the interview, she could wind up the whole thing. She picked up her purse and her clipboard from the adjoining seat and got out of the car, then walked up to the nearest door—it happened to be one of the new houses—and rang the door chimes. She'd grown accustomed enough to standing outside front doors so that the time didn't seem very long before the plywood, simulated Early American door opened.

"Yes?"

Carrie sized her up at once—married about a year, childless, sheltered life, and blasé. "Good morning," she said with a practiced embarrassed smile. "I'm Carrie Anderson interviewing for ARMBREWSTER RESEARCH. If you're not terribly busy right now, I'd like to interview you." This was opening number three and was always followed by an intense expression of hurting feet, gratitude, and enough reticence not to seem a saleswoman.

"I'm not doin' a damn thing," the young matron said. "C'mon in and fire away." She stood back and let Carrie pass into the richly-papered plasterboard foyer through to the L-shaped living room with the sliding glass doors to an as yet unbuilt patio and the short end of the L serving for dining space. "Boring, isn't it?" the girl ~id with a room-encompassing arm movement. She leaned forward and added in a stage whisper, "but terribly expensive."

"It's very nice," Carrie answered not quite sure of what to say.

"So's Grant's Tomb," she said. "Park your buns on one of those thousand-dollar settees . . . want some coffee? How about a drink . . . nothing like a noontime martini to give you the suburban feeling, is there?"

"Well, no, thank you, I, uh, I don't think I should." She was more than at a loss as to how to handle the situation. The girl was young, maybe twenty-four or twenty-five, and about Carrie's height—five foot five, or so—with short blond hair and deep-set gray eyes. Although her body was boyish, her face was full and Carrie couldn't help thinking of Sara as she watched her.

"C'mon. Keep me from feeling like a boozer. On the rocks, how's that." She'd already crossed over to a rather ostentatious bar on the far side of the room. "Like weak, huh? Nothing to upset the boss." Glasses and ice cubes appeared without effort.

"Well, all right," Carrie said and smiled inwardly at

what Mr. America Arnold would think of all this. "But a really weak one. I've not had lunch."

"Live, friend, live. I'll fix you some lunch too. What'd you say your name was?"

Carrie repeated it and for just a moment had a feeling of panic, an urgent need to run out of this house and away from that girl.

"Hi, Carrie. Mine's Kim Willis. *Mrs.* Willis, mustn't forget that. Live around here?" She handed Carrie her glass.

"Not too far. Near the college. Just down from the Daitch . . ."

"Gotya. I'd say married," she squinted at Carrie, "a kid or two, and runnin' around ringing doorbells to kill the time."

Carrie laughed. She couldn't help it. Kim, Mrs. Willis, despite her tough manner and blunt approach, was a baby, just a juvenile trying to cover up her fears and appear sophisticated like young swaggering boys using four-letter words. "You're close," she said, "the difference lies in motive or, let me amend that, in the way it's done rather than why or how it's done."

"Hey," Kim, Mrs. Willis said slowly sitting down on an antique replica chair across from Carrie, "you're *human!* You sure you're not pushing the Welcome Committee or something?"

"To New Rochelle?" Carrie said.

"You mean you don't think this town with its tidy little beach and one Negro per school is the living end?"

Carrie was beginning to enjoy herself immensely, and she'd barely sipped her drink. Kim was certainly something new in her life, arresting and a challenge. "If I have to think of New Rochelle at all," she answered, "I certainly would never want to think of it as 'the end'." She had no idea why she was saying these things, really, she'd never objected to New Rochelle in the least; if anything, quite the contrary.

"I'll be goddamned," Kim said. "What'd you do for kicks?"

"Push doorbells, just as you said."

"Is your husband in management consulting or whatever they call it?"

Carrie shook her head. "Advertising."

"Same crap anyway you slice it. Money?"

"We're not hungry."

Kim shrugged and rolled her eyes upward. "Mine's oaded. Came that way and keeps making more. Not milions, mind you, but less than fifty-grand a year makes him lervous. It kind of takes all the fun out of life, y'know vhat I mean?"

"Depends on whether you have to buy your fun or not," Carrie said and strived for a continental expression. Withmut meaning to she was somehow competing with Kim, lad to have the last quip. She watched the slim girl stand ind cross over to the bar, then return with the balance of he mixed martinis. She was wearing properly faded Levis ind a haltar-bra top. Carrie was terribly impressed with the smooth creamy skin so casually exposed, at the very small waist that left the Levis clinging to Kim's hips for support and the strong legs that kept the pants-legs taut. There wasn't an ounce of fat on Kim's body and yet she was not in the least skinny or bony; in fact, Carrie concluded in Paul's vernacular, she was a damn trim ship.

"C'mon, let's polish this off and then I'll put some peanut butter on a cracker and we'll make like housewives."

Rather than admit she might not handle two martinis very well, Carrie extended her glass with an air of daily routine. "You mix a good one," she said.

"Practice makes perfect," Kim said and there was an ironical glint in her eyes. "Make with the questionnaire and let's get that over with so we can talk. That clipboard of yours gives me the creeps."

Carrie smiled and leaned over to the coffee table where she'd placed it. She was very aware of her own body as she did so, aware that her blouse would be pulled tightly across her breasts to reveal their fullness, and pleased with herself that she did have nicer breasts than Kim; Kim's were sweet, as the expression goes, but Carrie's were sexy, womanly. "Ready?" she asked and sat up with her pencil poised.

"Anytime," she answered.

Carrie's mind partially froze at Kim's reply but she quickly dismissed the possible double entendre—not Kim, she just wasn't the type. "Do you take vitamins?"

Kim let out a loud guffaw. "Is that the pitch?" At Carrie's nodded reply, Kim tried to keep a straight face. "No."

Carrie checked off the No box. "That's good," she said sincerely. "You're the first person I've met who doesn't, and ARMBREWSTER always likes to see a few negative reports, the impartial approach, y'know."

"What a gas. . . ."

"Why don't you take them? Tell me slowly because I've got to write it in."

"What for? I'm healthy as a horse, have as much energy as a nuclear sub, and the cook makes very balanced dinners."

"Does your husband take them?"

"If it's a pill he takes it! Any kind. Takes so many half the time he sounds like a bolt factory."

"Yes," Carrie said, "but does he take vitamins?"

"How the hell do I know," Kim said. "Hold on, I'll go look in the medicine cabinet." She got up and left the room, then returned shortly with a medium-size bottle. "These vitamins?"

Carrie took the bottle and read the label. "Just Vitamin C. Probably takes them for colds. That's all there was?"

Kim shrugged. "Take a year to read all the labels in there, but that's the only one I saw at a glance that had the word vitamin on it."

"That's close enough I guess. Now," she pulled out two 5 by 7 cards with a single paragraph of copy printed on them. "I'm going to read you what's on these cards and you tell me which one agrees most with your viewpoint." She read aloud that the average family does not have a balanced diet and therefore needed a vitamin supplement, with some other pithy words on the subject, and the other card was the reverse.

"You asking what I think the rest of the country does, or what I do?"

"Well, either one. Give me both," Carrie smiled and looked up at Kim. She was sitting with one leg hung over the arm of the chair and the other stretched out before her—a bird's eye view of Kim's crotch made all the more suggestive by the seam in her dungarees. Carrie quickly looked back at her clipboard. The interview went on for about another fifteen minutes and then Carrie straightened up and stood. "Well, that does it. Thanks a lot, Mrs. Willis."

"Where you going? I thought we were going to have lunch?" Kim got out of her chair so lithely that it was like a single motion. "And the name's Kim. Why so formal? We've shared noonday martinis together, remember?"

Carrie laughed, but she had to get out of that house. Kim was making her very nervous and fidgety. Carrie wasn't too sure why, but she had no intentions of analyzing it—it might not be safe. "Sorry, Kim, but I've got a lot more stops to make before the kids come home from school. I'd love to stay," she said, "I really would, and this has been the most fun-interview I've done yet. . . ."

"But the mundane world beckons, huh?"

"Something like that. I took on the job, and I have to finish it."

"Then there's the old man's dinner to fix, right?" Kim was looking at her as if she'd suddenly grown a third eye.

"Well, not tonight," Carrie answered a little surprised at Kim's direct personal questions. "My husband's out of town."

"That's a break," Kim said. "Or do you miss him?"

"Aren't you worried that someday someone's going to cut off your long nose?" Carrie said with a friendly laugh.

Kim's face suddenly became very serious. "You're right, Carrie. I'm sorry. I get so bored I forget my manners and come on too strong. Gang Busters Willis, they call me."

"That's all right, I wasn't offended or anything."

There was a short silence between them as if they were both thinking of hundreds of things to say by way of further explanation and knew any of them would sound ridiculous. "Well, I'd better get going. Thanks again, Kim, and maybe we could get together for that lunch one of these days."

"Sure," Kim said rather moodily and followed Carrie to the front door. "We'll get together."

Carrie opened the door and stepped out into the harsh sunlight, walked down to the street and started for the house next door. She turned once, just on impulse, and saw Kim standing in the doorway watching her. Carrie waved at her and laughed when Kim thumbed her nose. It had been a strange experience all right, Carrie thought as she pushed the next doorbell, and somehow she knew that she would see Kim again. It was an exciting idea and it would be nice to have a friend, someone you could be honest with and not worry about being a bit unorthodox or using a few swearwords.

Chapter IV

Carrie had not been able to finish up the vitamin job that same day. Somehow, after her meeting with Kim, she hadn't been able to really concentrate on the job; her stethoscope on the pulse of America seemed to be out of whack. The housewives who did open their door to her were indeed "stale, flat and unprofitable." So she gave up around one-thirty and drove home to take a nap before the kids came home from school. A nap after noonday martinis was just the thing, she decided in a state of lethargy and numbness she couldn't remember having had before in her entire life. Midday drinking had never been one of her fortes and she wished to hell she hadn't had the second martini.

It had been a different kind of Tuesday and she was glad that she'd have that night alone to think about it— provided she could stay awake long enough. Luckily, the kids had not been any exceptional bother, no mishaps, and by eight o'clock both were in bed, if not asleep. Carrie finished up the dishes and thought a hair of the dog might come in nicely at that point. She poured herself a pony of Paul's brandy and sank into his chair in the living room, got up and turned on the TV and went back to her chair. It was an old Motorola set and she lived in constant suspense between viewings if it'd last another night. These were the only times Carrie would watch TV without something special being on; when Paul was gone and just to relax a bit before bedtime. She always went to bed early when he was gone. After a few *ppfffts* and *bloops* the picture came in on the set and by some miracle needed no adjusting. It was one of those weekly detective programs— of which there can be nothing worse, Carrie believed—and she'd caught it in the midst of a good-guy bad-guy brawl, followed by a commercial proving that the manufacturer's product was inadequate since they had now come out with a superior one, and the program resumed with a summary of the entire show and the hero nicely rejecting the young girl—a young girl, Carrie noticed, who bore a remarkable resemblance to Kim Willis. An odd girl, Carrie thought. So desperate to make an impression of the worst kind. Kim certainly couldn't have really meant half the things she said, about her husband or her home or her life. So caustic and defensive. People just don't talk that way if they really mean it, she thought and decided that perhaps she might have a good influence on Kim, a settling one. The girl was barely more than a child, emotionally anyway, and maybe all she needed was someone to help her grow up, to accept her responsibilities. She'd wait a few days and stop by again, just to prove that she really had enjoyed herself if nothing else.

The next day, Wednesday, Carrie got the kids off to school—it was a troop-meeting day for Sambo who looked especially handsome in his uniform—and dressed for her "rounds" as she had come to call them. Without particularly thinking about it she automatically drove back to the same neighborhood to complete her interviews; she always worked a neighborhood until she'd exhausted it and saved a lot of needless running around and time that way. She parked about five houses up this time and got out of the car. Her luck was exceptionally good—perhaps it was the early hour while housewives were relaxing over a quiet cup of coffee after getting their families off to work and school —and by 11:30 she'd covered enough houses to make it worthwhile to return to the car and drive it up further. Five or six more interviews should really do it, she decided walking back in the warm morning sunlight. It was a lovely day, a quiet one except for the reassuring distant sound of someone cutting a lawn. A light breeze played in her hair, and the pavement under her flat-heeled shoes had that special sponginess of late summer. Everything had a crisp shininess to it, greens were richer, browns more golden, and everything had a well-edged, defined look as if she'd suddenly stepped into a world of 3-D technicolor. She wondered briefly whatever had happened to 3-D and recalled some awful film she'd seen starring Vincent Price where she had to wear those uncomfortable glasses that kept slipping off. All she could remember of it now was that there'd been a tremendous fire and that she'd thought at the time that it was a dreadful waste of lovely antique furniture. She supposed that Hollywood made substitutions for scenes like that, props, or something, but she could never get used to it . . . especially when they'd show cars going over cliffs, always new convertibles that she'd love to own. She always felt so sorry for her little Volkswagen; it always sounded as if she were working it too hard with its little loud engine faithfully trying to keep up with her gas pedal demands.

She spotted her car standing all alone on the street and thought she might wash it so it could feel proud of itself, then smiled at herself for being so silly. As Carrie reached its side and opened the door, she was startled to hear, "Hi!"

She looked quickly in the back seat and saw Kim scrunched down in it with her legs resting on the side of the car. "Well, hello," Carrie answered more than a little surprised and undecided whether she should be annoyed or be pleased. "What're you doing in there?"

Kim reached down casually and brought up a large paper bag. "Lunch," she grinned. "I owed you. Saw you drive up, made a few sandwiches, and thought we'd run down to Davenport Park for a picnic."

Carrie had to laugh. "How long have you been waiting there like that?" The idea of lunch did appeal to her; she'd not bothered with breakfast that morning.

"Not long. I saw you coming back toward the car and just hopped in." She stuck her hand into her large straw purse and pulled out a bottle. "See what I bought? It's my peace offering for being such a nosy bitch yesterday."

"I don't sell vitamins," Carrie smiled. "I just poll 'em."

"Shouldn't be a total loss. George'll be delighted and think I'm worried about him. Hungry?"

"As the proverbial bear," Carrie said. "Are you going to stay back there or are you coming up front."

Kim swung her legs down on the floor and pushed the seat forward to climb out. "How can you stand this egg you drive," she asked sitting down in front. "Goddamn hardtop roller skate!"

"You could always walk, or run alongside. . . ."

Kim grinned impishly. "I'm on good behavior, treat me nice."

Carrie didn't say anything but found herself very flattered that Kim liked her enough to try to please her. She started up the engine and drove to the end of the street, then made a right turn. The large gravel parking area was deserted and she switched off the engine. They just sat in the car for a moment looking out over the expanse of green lawn and trees with the Long Island Sound beyond the cliff—rocks, really, but Carrie preferred to think of them as something more romantic. It was a lovely view and the only thing that marred it were the barely visible beach cabanas of the private clubs on either side of the park, and of course, dingy Fort Slocum on its penitentiary-like island about a mile off the coast line.

"How'd you like that," Kim said with a touch of the old toughness in her voice.

"What?"

"That *sign!* No dogs, picnics, don't pick the flowers, stay off the lawn, no swimming, no bicycles . . . what next? Might as well tell a whore to stay away from men!"

Carrie laughed. "Your similes are really rather unique, Kim." Worried that Kim might think her a conforming chicken, she added, "There doesn't seem to be anyone around, though. We could walk down to the rocks and have our lunch there."

"Great! Let's go." Kim jumped out of the car and wrapped her left arm around the shopping bag tightly and carried her purse in her right hand letting it swing with her movements.

It was a rather long walk to the rocks, perhaps a half mile or more, and the grass was still wet with dew despite the warm sun. They walked it leisurely, not saying anything except once when Carrie offered to help carry the lunch. Kim had simply shaken her head. She walked with her face raised to the sun like an animal following a scent, and the unbroken breeze in the park tossed her short locks of hair in all directions. She seemed so much more at peace out there, and Carrie again noticed how very much a child she looked, and wondered if Kim would have that special sunny and sweet smell to her Sara had. She liked Kim the way she was now, quiet and pensive, youthful and uncomplicated, and particularly the absence of sarcasm verbally or even in carriage. It was a shame that people had to have voices, Carrie thought. They should be like animals so that you could appreciate them by gesture and physical beauty alone. People say such petty things, make themselves ugly with cruel words and flippant jokes. Kim, in the sunlight with the salty breeze all around them, reminded Carrie of a fawn. There was a strange innocent and awkward air about her that made Carrie feel very protective and worldly.

They reached the edge of the grass and started over the rocks. A thick, continuing white line had been painted on them with white letters blocked every few feet reading: DON'T CROSS THIS LINE. Both girls looked at each other, back at the warning, and then began to giggle like children hiding in a corner away from the rest of the world. "At least they let us breathe," Kim said as they made their way down the rocks to the water line.

"Shh," Carrie said, "somebody'll hear you and post a sign."

They found a nice flattened stone a few yards away and sat down. Carrie worried a moment about getting her skirt dirty, but promptly forgot about it in the peace and quiet of their chosen spot. "Tide's still in," Carrie said.

"Um-hm," Kim answered absently. She rolled open the top of the bag and pulled out a folded piece of wax paper which she deftly unfolded and spread between them. Then four sandwiches, two on rye and two on white, a jar of kosher pickles, and a quart of beer still cold enough for the frost to be on the sides. "Hope you like beer. It's all I brought."

"Love it," Carrie answered and suddenly realized she hadn't had any beer in a long time. She wondered why. She used to drink enough of it when she went out to the clubs . . . but she didn't want to think about that. She watched Kim stand up and prop another bottle of beer between two rocks where the water was. Kim stood looking out over the water with her back turned to Carrie. She had on her dungarees again, and sneakers that had about finished their last sneak, but was wearing a soft white cotton blouse with a scoop-neck and little buttons all around the bottom of it.

"What bridge is that?" Kim asked.

Carrie leaned forward and peered past her. "The White-stone, I think. Careful you don't fall. . . ."

Kim swung slowly from the waist and looked at her. "Me? I'm the original mountain goat." She smiled strangely as she came back, sat down, and opened the beer. "My mother used to say that when I was learning to walk I never fell down once."

"That might be a mother's exaggeration," Carrie said.

"Where are you from? Originally, I mean." She took the sandwich Kim offered her and looked inside to see what it was, then took a bite. It was good; boiled ham with lots of mayonnaise and mustard, and even catsup. She should've known that Kim would goop up a sandwich but had to admit it was exceptionally tasty.

"Arrumpsbldtg," Kim answered.

"Where?"

Kim swallowed. "Warrensburg. It's a small dump in upstate New York. Lots of country, no action."

"I like the country," Carrie said then leaned back on one elbow, not too comfortably.

"I don't. I like the seaside. I'd like to live in Maine, or maybe San Francisco so you could have the ocean and a big city both."

"That's just because you were raised in the country."

"Maybe. I don't know. I get tired of the country, you know what I mean? It doesn't change fast enough for me. But the ocean's always changing." She finished off her sandwich and was starting on the second. "These are better," she said to herself with approval. "Liverwurst."

Carrie smiled. She was just starting on the second half of her first sandwich. "You eat too fast, like a kid. You're going to get ulcers." She reached over for the bottle and took a swallow of beer. It was cold and tasted particularly good with the out-of-doors and salt air.

"Can't get ulcers unless you worry. I've nothing to worry about." There was a trace of sarcasm in her voice but hardly noticeable. "Where are you from."

"North Bergen, New Jersey," Carrie answered and waited for some wisecrack, but none came.

Kim's head tilted a little to one side. "Isn't that where they have all the slaughterhouses and packing companies?"

"That's right," Carrie answered and sat up to get her circulation going in her arm.

"Have another sandwich," Kim prompted.

"No thanks, that's more than I usually eat."

"G'on."

"No, really."

"All right," Kim said with a slight shrug. "I'll eat it." She picked up the bottle and swallowed about half a pint before putting it down. "I drove through there once."

"North Bergen?"

Kim nodded. "It looked awfully depressing. Were you poor?"

"No, not really. My dad worked for one of the packing companies and you didn't have economical track housing then. Considering what many families went through during the depression, we did quite well. A lot of the kids were on relief. The ladies used to come around with baskets of food and used clothes for them to wear." Carrie laughed softly. "I can remember envying them and thinking it was very exciting. Funny."

Kim smiled. "I know what you mean. A boy in my class broke his leg once and I remember I thought it was terribly dramatic, with that limp 'n all, and the special attention he got."

"I missed the depression in a way," Carrie went on. "I mean, I was too young when it was at its worst to really know what was going on."

"Your family still alive?" Kim asked.

"My dad died. Mother went to live with my sister in Atlantic City. Yours?"

"Yeah," Kim said and her mouth twisted into an ugly grimace. "They've both remarried . . . my mother twice. Suppose my dad would get another divorce but he can't afford all that alimony. He's an insurance claims adjuster, makes pretty good money but not enough for that."

It was the first insight Carrie had been able to get out of Kim, and a rather telling one. A broken home a child might be able to understand as the years went by, but not multiple marriages or the knowledge that marriage is inevitably a sour lot. She wondered why Kim, under the circumstances, should marry a man she didn't respect. One would've thought that she'd be the type to wait for real love and settle for nothing less. But she didn't want to pry. And anyway, it was probably just Kim's brittle sarcasm that made her sound as if she didn't like her husband; a defense mechanism against getting hurt. Carrie began to wad up the wrappers and napkins and put them into the bag. "Aren't you going to finish my sandwich?" she asked.

"I don't want it anymore," Kim said, and tossed it into the sack as if it were so much mush. She raised both her arms and put her hands behind her head, arching her back and stretching. "Guess I lose interest too fast," she added and giggled mischievously.

"Well, it's back to work for me, I guess." Carrie avoided Kim's eyes afraid of finding some plea to stay on; she didn't think she could've refused. "Don't forget the other bottle."

"Hell," Kim said harshly. "Leave it for some poor bastard wino to find. I don't feel like lugging it back." She stood up abruptly and threw her wadded paper napkin into the ocean, then stood defiantly watching it bob and finally submerge. "Let's split."

It disturbed Carrie that Kim should so carelessly throw trash into so lovely a place but she put it down to more of Kim's compulsive aggression. She didn't say anything. Kim started back up the rocks and Carrie followed carrying the bag of trash, which she neatly deposited in the nearest litter basket. Kim didn't wait for her, but just kept on walking toward the car so that there were a good five or six yards between them the whole way. By the time Carrie reached the car, Kim was slumped in the bucket seat smoking a cigarette as if they were going out of style.

"Your husband still out of town?" Kim asked as Carrie got in.

"Yes." She didn't have the vaguest idea what Kim was leading up to. In fact, if Kim suggested they should rob a bank it wouldn't have surprised her.

"How about a movie tonight? Mine's going to a lodge dinner. The Proctor's got a double horror film on, might be kicks."

"Well," Carrie hesitated. "It's hard for me to get out evenings. I'd have to get a baby sitter and they're not easy to find on short notice."

"Haven't you got a neighbor or someone?"

Carrie thought it best not to mention that she hated to ask Elaine Henderson to sit unless it was terribly important, that Elaine had kids of her own and it wasn't any fun for her, so she lied. "No, not tonight. My neighbor's going out."

"There's got to be *some*body!" She said it impatiently, a sharp demand in her voice.

"I'll call a few sitters when I get home," Carrie said "but don't count on it. I mean, if you find someone else to go with . . ."

"Nah. They're all a bunch of creeps around here. I'll call you around six-thirty and check with you then."

"Do you know my number. . . ." Carrie began feeling as if she were letting the team down.

"In the book?"

"Yes."

"I'll find it. How many ways can you spell Anderson?"

Carrie didn't answer but started up the car and drove Kim home. She let the engine run as Kim got out. "Thanks for the lunch, Kim, it was . . ."

"Never mind," Kim said with a slow smile. "And I'm sorry if I jumped down your throat about the movies. We don't have to go tonight."

"But I'd like to," Carrie heard herself say unexpectedly and marveled at how Kim could so easily maneuver her.

"Well, I'll call you later. Your car or mine?"

"Oh, I don't care," Carrie said. "Let's not worry about that until we know we're going."

Kim shrugged. "Okay. See you later." She lingered a second at the closed door, then walked off up the path to her house. Carrie followed her with her eyes until she was in the door, then released the clutch and slowly drove down the street to where she'd been headed before finding Kim in the back seat.

Chapter V

Three weeks went by after that day, three strange and undefinable weeks for Carrie. She had managed to find a sitter that night but had had to call on an elderly woman she didn't like to have sit because she was hard of hearing. But she figured the children would be safe for one night with her, and Sambo was old enough to take care of Sara if anything happened, and she just didn't have the heart to have to tell Kim "No" when she called. She might have taken it personally and Carrie didn't want that. Kim had picked her up in a new Ford convertible and they'd driven up Main Street on the off-chance of finding a place to park, but finally gave up and parked on Huguenot with its old, dark stores and noisy bars. Carrie would've preferred to put the car in a lot and pay rather than have to come out of a late movie and walk over to Huguenot Street, but she was afraid Kim would tease her. The films had been incredibly bad but Kim seemed to enjoy herself, enjoy making snide comments during the film—something Carrie normally detested and one reason she rarely went to the movies, but which for some reason struck her as very amusing that night. On their way home, Carrie asked Kim if she'd like to come in for a cup of coffee before going on home, but Kim had said "No, not yet," in a peculiar kind of way, as if Carrie's home might hold frightening memories for her.

Contrary to what Carrie had expected, she didn't hear from Kim right away. And several days went by without any communication between them. Carrie wondered if perhaps Kim was expecting her to make the first move, but doubted it; Kim was a strange, moody girl and would call when she was ready to be with people again, she was sure of that. But Paul came back on Thursday and by then Carrie had a new assignment—a Chinese food company—

48

and though she certainly hadn't forgotten about Kim, she didn't have much time to dwell upon her. That Saturday Paul had called Carrie to the phone saying some woman was asking for her, had she paid the gas bill. Carrie picked up the receiver. "Yes?"

"Mrs. Anderson?" the familiar girlish voice of Kim asked. "This is Mrs. Willis."

"How do you do, Mrs. Willis," Carrie said with an even tone.

"Just reporting to let you know that I detest telephones and only use them during an emergency—something that has never occurred in my life—and to make appointments."

"I see. Well, I quite understand," Carrie said and put up her hand to Paul's "Who the hell are you talking to, what's that all about."

"I'm so glad. Some people might interpret it as being antisocial."

"Not at all. Is this in the nature of an appointment?"

"Loosely speaking. Macy's having a sale Monday and I thought you might like to go up to White Plains and shop a bit, and we could have lunch out somewhere quiet."

"Just a moment, Mrs. Willis," Carrie said, "I'll have to check my schedule." She used the British pronunciation. "Yes. Monday would be fine. Are they sale-ing anything in particular?"

"The usual. Washcloths and 99¢ house tools. But it should be a curious adventure to watch the Westchesterites congregate."

"No doubt. We must make it early though so I can be back . . ."

". . . in time for the children. I'll pick you up around ten-ish," Kim said, "disgusting hour that it is."

"Fine. See you then." Carrie hung up and turned to see Paul standing right behind her with a churlish scowl of not being kept informed. It struck her then that she hadn't mentioned meeting Kim, not a word. She supposed it was only because she didn't think he'd be interested and then sat down with him and explained who Kim was and

49

how they'd met. It was a very brief explanation, and she didn't bother to tell him anything about Kim's moodiness or her sarcasm; didn't bother, or simply censored it subconsciously as she knew that Paul probably wouldn't like that type of person.

That Monday went by and they had an exceptionally pleasant time together. They laughed a great deal and Kim was in very high spirits the whole time. Carrie had to work the next two days but Thursday they took a drive down to City Island and snacked on tough, greasy clams and shrimp, poked around the few streets and then re-returned home to Kim's house for a mid-afternoon martini. The following week they saw each other about every other day, going for walks along the shore and collecting mussels, or passing a half-hour or more with Frances in her Pottery Shop on Main Street—the only other non-creep in New Rochelle, as Kim put it—and just in general getting to know each other better, though Kim never referred to her childhood or her parents. Mostly they just sat around, not talking a great deal but listening to Kim's records on her expensive hi fi set—a Garrard turntable with an rpm adjuster, and all the other impressive looking components inclusive of a Tandberg stereo tape recorder—and sipping martinis. Carrie was getting quite accustomed to those martinis and each time she swore she'd refuse and have something else, but each time Kim would ignore her mild protest and mix it anyway. By the third week there was a very definite bond between them very much like the fast friendships of adolescent girls who can't be apart, and when they are can't wait to see each other to reveal every detail of what had happened during their separation. Yet even with this closeness, Carrie still knew very little about Kim's background or her present intimate life. And, in turn, she herself was reluctant to confide details about herself assuming that if Kim wanted to know she'd ask point-blank.

Paul had commented several times on what a good effect her new friendship was having on Carrie, that she seemed more animated, more . . . well, *younger,* if she knew what he meant. And Carrie did. She could feel it herself; there was a buoyancy she'd not felt since . . . since those first years out of high school when she'd gone into that other world. Coincidence, no doubt, that's all it could be, she rationalized. This was a change of pace for her, a new life in a way, just as it had been then and that's all there was to it. And, in a way, she had been just as tough and sassy at that stage as Kim was now. She knew what it was to have to "put down" everything—as Kim said—so that nothing could reach her or hurt her. But after her first love —had it really happened?—she'd toned down, and by the second love she was more adult, and with the termination of the third affair she knew she'd have to stop all the non-sense, grow up and live a more secure, quieter life. The other way just didn't last. Why, she didn't know; only that it didn't. And the other way meant that there could never be any children and she wanted children as she matured more. The other way offered nothing but heartache and an empty old age. She'd seen too many cases and knew it was true ninety-eight percent of the time. So perhaps Kim too had to learn—not in the same way of course because Kim didn't have her old problem—to relax within herself and accept herself. She'd tone down yet; she already had quite a bit just in the short while knowing Carrie. It felt good to be able to think of it as her "old problem", like a case of juvenile acne long gone and with it the sensitivity about it.

Early in October the two girls decided that their husbands should meet, that they should meet each other's respective husbands as well. And Kim came up with the idea of having a party.

"You bring two couples of your friends, and we'll have two couples of George's friends," Kim said. "We'll have it at our house, George can afford it better."

"Well, frankly, I don't think we know two couples who'd enjoy a party," Carrie stalled. She had no idea what Kim thought a party should be like and she didn't relish the idea of bringing along some of Paul's staid business associates to something quite so impulsive. "But we'll share the booze cost anyway."

"Does Paul like parties? George hates them," Kim giggled, "that is until his fifth shot. Then he picks up."

"Paul's about the same way. He seems to think that a party's an excuse to get good and drunk. Not sloppy," she added hastily, but, well, kind of silly."

"I dig," Kim said. "Sounds more and more as if Paul and George should've married each other." She laughed loudly at her joke and gave Carrie a knowing wink.

Carrie hoped it wasn't *too* knowing a wink. "Well, let's hope that they like each other."

"Why?" Kim asked with an aloof gesture. "Who needs 'em? Have more fun without 'em, don't we?"

Carrie was getting very uncomfortable with the turn of the conversation. "They come in handy for some things, physically speaking," she answered and forced a lurid smirk.

Kim shrugged. "I hear tell," she leaned over toward Carrie, "that there are women who manage without 'em." She laughed again and tweaked Carrie on the cheek.

"What about canapes," Carrie said quickly. "Or should we have a buffet?"

"Hell, let's have it catered. I don't want to sweat all day getting things ready for our own party. Like we are the guests of honor in a manner of speaking, aren't we? The party's for our benefit."

"That gets terribly expensive and it's a waste of money."

"George's money, doll, good ol' George's. He writes it off on his income tax."

Carrie smiled. "I can see him offering advice to Paul on his management problems," she said, "Paul and his one secretary and one lay-out artist."

"Potential, darling, potential! Paul may turn out to be another BBD&O one day."

"Do you mind if I don't count on it?" Carrie said. They discussed what kind of a party it should be, dress or informal, and decided on cocktail dresses, and just a dark suit for the men. Kim was adamant about having it catered and Carrie finally gave in, and they decided to make it one week from that day since it was a Friday and everyone could sleep late the next morning and nurse their heads. Kim played with the idea of a masquerade party, but Carrie dissuaded her saying she'd never get Paul to go.

Carrie went home with genuine mixed feelings; she wasn't at all sure how Paul was going to react to the idea of a party but she couldn't anticipate any real resistance. After all this time he was bound to be just a little curious about his wife's new friend . . . wasn't he? Oh well, time enough to find out this evening, she concluded. As soon as she was inside the door she began calling baby sitters. Strategy No. 1: "But I already have a sitter!" Then, that accomplished, she went to the bedroom closet and took out her cocktail dress. She tried it on and decided it should be shortened by about an inch and most definitely cleaned. No. 2: "But I've already taken my dress to the cleaners, and shortened it, and everything." By the end of the afternoon she had a fortress of arguments inclusive of proposing to Paul that he buy himself a new suit. She smiled at how she knew he'd react. Paul always complained that he hated to shop, but it was only a token gesture of masculine protest. Actually he loved it and always felt very pleased with himself afterwards, even strutted a little with his new feathers. Yes, a new suit was definitely in order.

Since it was their day for dinner out, Carrie didn't mention the party to Paul until they were comfortably seated at the Holiday restaurant in Mount Vernon, with a well-chilled martini in front of them.

Paul toyed with his glass contentedly, then looked up at Carrie with a boyish expression. "You look awfully pretty tonight, Mrs. Anderson."

"Why, thank you," she said. "You look as if you thought it improper for a husband to say such a thing," she smiled and recognized a hint of a Kim-ism in her tone. But he laughed and raised his glass in a toast before taking the first sip.

"What's with the martini?" he said. "Tired of brandy Alexanders?"

"All businesswomen drink martinis," she said with a raised eyebrow pose. "Paul. . . ."

"Um-hm?"

"Kim and I were talking today. . . ."

"Oh, d'you see each other again today?"

Even though he said it casually, Carrie automatically became somewhat on guard. "Yes, I was in the area and stopped by for coffee."

"Can't imagine what you two find to talk about all the time," he said, a patient male vs. female look on his face. "You two must see each other about every day."

"Not *that* often," Carrie said lightly. "But that's what I was leading up to."

"What?"

"That we've become such good friends and all and that you two haven't met, and I haven't met George. . . ."

"George is her husband?"

"Yes, and that neither you nor George have met. . . ."

"George Willis, George Willis. He wouldn't be the same George Willis of Willis, Kingsley and Kingsley, would he?"

"Yes, dear, he is. I told you that a long time ago."

"Guess I wasn't paying attention. Ol' George Willis, eh?"

"Now, Paul. Let me finish, will you?"

"Oh sure. What were you saying?"

She could see his brain still clucking over "ol' George". "I was saying that Kim and I were discussing the fact that it would be nice if we all got together and met each other."

"Good idea," Paul said, "we'll have to do that some-time."

"Well," Carrie said trying to keep the impatience out of her voice, "Kim and I thought we'd have a little party, nothing too fancy, just a little get-together."

"That'd be nice," Paul answered absently. "Want another martini?"

"Yes, please. Well, we made a tentative arrangement for this coming Friday."

"Friday what?"

"The party, Paul, this coming Friday."

"Gee, hon, I don't know about that. I'd been sort of

putting off telling you, until I knew for sure I'd really have to go, but I've just got to get out and see some of the accounts. Probably be gone about ten days or so."

It felt very strange to Carrie to not be in the least concerned about his being away for so long, but then she had her job and Kim and there was plenty to keep her busy. "Well, when would you have to leave?"

"I was thinking of going next week, but I suppose I could put it off. A couple of days isn't going to put me out of business," he grinned, "and we haven't been to a party in a long time. Kind of like to meet George Willis, too. You never know when someone like that can be a big help in business; see his name a lot in *Ad Age;* he's really got a future cut out."

"Yes, and I thought you might like a new suit and now, especially, if you're going on a business trip."

"You know how I hate to shop, hon. If it's going to be that big an affair, maybe you could go without me, you know, my husband's on a business trip and all that."

"Now, Paul. . . ."

"Well, we'll talk about it later on, all right?" He picked up the menu, forced a nonchalance about the prices, and studied it carefully. "Shrimp cocktail first, same as always?" he asked.

"Of course, and I'll have whatever you're having," she said demurely. Carrie believed that honey catches more flies than vinegar.

*   *   *   *

They paused at the front door before ringing the bell and could already hear the music. It was an almost cool evening for October, a perfect kind of night for a party especially after the alcohol began to raise everyone's temperature. "My tie straight?" Paul asked and fingered it tentatively.

Carrie smiled and fidgeted with the knot just to please him. "It's not a bow tie, darling, of course it's straight."

He pushed the bell nervously. "Sometimes the knot goes

55

off, y'know? I don't think we should've paid so much for this suit, though."

"It looks very nice on you, darling, and you've earned it."

The door swung open and a maid let them in, took Carrie's wrap and Paul's hat, and led them into the living room. "Great house," Paul whispered as they walked in and Carrie had trouble keeping a smile off her face knowing how Kim felt about it. "I'd like us to have a maid some day," he added.

"She's just for tonight, so don't worry," Carrie answered in the same whisper, although she couldn't for the life of her think of why she should whisper.

"All the same . . ."

"Hi there!" Kim called, greeting them from the door that led to the den. "We're in here." She walked up to Paul and gave him a candid appraisal. "Hm. Tall, dark . . . very successful looking, and brooding. I adore brooding men, it makes me so maternal." She smiled impishly and put her arm through Paul's. "I'm Kim Willis, abductress of your spouse."

Carrie winced imperceptibly at that, she didn't know how Paul would take it. "Which spouse?" she said to make it clearly a joke; Paul wasn't very subtle.

He laughed a little uncertainly but allowed himself to be led into the den with Carrie behind him. "Well," Paul said, "I'll be willingly abducted. I can resist anything but women." His eyes took in her young shoulders and breasts.

Carrie looked at her too. And Kim certainly did look wonderful in a deep red strapless dress with a very full skirt that rustled as she walked. Carrie wasn't in the least surprised to see that Kim had already taken off her shoes—if she'd ever had them on. She must be wearing a padded bra, Carrie thought, not in the least catty but just amused, since Kim's breasts raised softly over the top of her dress. They looked warm and inviting in the dimly lit den, with shadows playing across them making it nearly impossible to take your eyes away. Carrie was glad she'd not had her dress dyed as she had momentarily thought to do. The pleated white folds of the Grecian style accentuated her own full breasts and somehow made her skin look tan, more dramatic and confident of her own allure, even though it gave the benefit of a wide V-cleavage almost to her waist.

She spotted George standing like a bourbon ad next to the empty fireplace. He was about her own height in high heels, thinning dark hair, but quite young—thirty-two or thirty-three, she guessed—and had a very athletic solid build. His features were regular, except for very deep set green eyes that gave him a sinister, hard look. He stared at her as she entered behind Paul and Kim, and instead of her usual embarrassment when anyone noticed her, she felt very pleased and sophisticated. She was within five feet of him when he finally spoke.

"You're an extremely lovely woman, Carrie, Kim hadn't mentioned that." His voice was unusually deep and sounded as if he had spent a good deal of time cultivating it, and his smile exposed an even row of very white small teeth, almost like a puppy's. He took a step forward and extended his free right hand. "Martini, Scotch, bourbon? What'll it be?"

"Martini, but on the rocks, thanks," she anwered pitching her voice to match his, and grateful for once that she normally did have a soft, low voice anyway. She thought he was laying on the Lord of the manor routine a bit thick but that it would probably go away after he relaxed a little. "Have you met my husband?" she said pointedly as he casually put his arm on her back.

Paul turned around and smiled down at George. "I've heard a great deal about you," he said as they shook hands. Carrie wished he hadn't said it.

"Not from your wife, I'm sure," George answered and looked at her meaningfully.

"Oh, no," Paul laughed. *"Ad Age,* and on the links. You don't belong to the Pelham Club, do you?"

Kim made a behind-the-back gesture to Carrie of "What, him?"

"Tennis is my game," George said. "Tennis, or a good workout at the Harvard Club. Never could understand this mania for chasing little balls around, especially when there are so many better things to chase." He looked over at Carrie and let his eyes rest on her breasts.

Conceited little snot, she thought, but immediately put it out of her mind. Probably just bravado, she decided, and sincerely hoped so for Kim's sake, at least.

"Well, it's relaxing for some of us," Paul went on and followed George to the temporary bar they'd set up in the den. "Besides, why chase when so many will come to you?" he joked. Paul frowned momentarily at the martini George mixed for Carrie, then handed it to her with a good-natured laugh. "I'm beginning to think our wives are sneaking the booze behind our backs, George. My wife never drank martinis before. . . ."

George didn't look up but poured two glasses of Scotch for them. "I *know* mine does," he said softly but loud enough with his voice's resonance to carry throughout the room. "It's her life," he added tonelessly.

"Seems that everyone in suburbia has a cocktail or two before dinner," Paul said uncomfortably and glanced at Carrie for some kind of reassurance.

George walked around the bar and sat down opposite Carrie. "Understand you two met during a vitamin run, or something."

"Or something," Carrie said with a wry smile.

The door chimes rang and the sound of a man's voice calling for Kim boomed through the house. "Where the hell are ya, you little vixen?" A huge-boned, angular man stormed into the den with a puff of a wife dressed all in black trailing in behind him, like a pigeon following a whale. *"There* you are! Hiya George. Still living in this squalor, huh?" He went over to Kim and lifted her bodily out of her seat with a big bear hug and planted a noisy kiss on her lips. Kim laughed genially.

"Richard Kingsley," George said flatly by way of an overall introduction, "my partner."

Carrie was first taken aback a little at Kingsley's entrance, and then unreasonably angry that he should be so familiar with Kim. This coupled with the fact that George wasn't gracious enough to bother to introduce Kingsley's wife put her in a darker mood than she'd care to admit. And she was more than irked with Kim for not only allowing that Kingsley creature to paw her, but worse to make it so evident that she enjoyed it. So this was Kim's life. Baboon men and invisible women. No wonder the poor thing was miserable, and sarcastic, and just in general unhappy. The poor thing just didn't have anyone to talk to or turn to . . . the poor thing. . . .

"I'm Mrs. Kingsley," a small voice piped into Carrie's ear and sat down so lightly Carrie could scarcely believe anyone was next to her. "Joan," she tittered, "Joan is what everyone calls me."

I could think of a few better names, Carrie thought, but caught herself in time. "I'm Carrie Anderson," she introduced herself and then Paul.

"Are you part of the Nation Carries?" Joan asked and giggled.

"JOan!" Richard Kingsley boomed. "Cut it out. Let me at least have a drink first." He shook Paul's hand and then Carrie's. "Don't mind my wife, she likes to think she's funny," he said and laughed loudly slamming a fist into Paul's arm. "Dick's the name. Glad to meet you. You look more like friends of Kim's," Dick Kingsley whispered, "George hasn't got any. Isn't she a riot though? Isn't she the best thing since television?" he said and pulled Kim over to his side and hugged her so hard Carrie was afraid Kim's breasts would pop out of her dress.

The brute! Carrie thought and wished to hell Kim would do something to get his big hairy paws off of her. She really couldn't understand how Kim could put up with him and had a disgusting image of Dick Kingsley unzipping his fly and peeing all over the furniture. He'd have a long, skinny penis, she just knew it, and probably just one ball too. She'd never loathed anyone so much on a first meeting in all her life. If she were George, or any man, she'd push his teeth down his throat!

"How about some music here," Dick yelled, "Let's have some dancing." He did a little jig and then leaned over and picked Kim up and started to carry her toward the living room where the hi-fi was.

Kim just had time to say "That's why I don't wear shoes," before he had her through the door, and she laughed gaily at how easily he held her. Idiots! Carrie swore to herself. All of them—idiots! Leftover Valentinos and Fairbanks Srs. What do they know about women, about how to treat a woman. She was furious until her eyes fell on Paul. He was standing near her holding his glass trying desperately to look as if he went to this kind of party all the time, nothing to it. She softened as she looked at him; he at least was a gentleman, in the real sense of the word. Oh, he could be stuffy sometimes, but it was a blessing compared to the slobs she'd seen tonight. From some hidden corner a speaker was turned on and bump-and-grind music blared into the den. Through the louver doors pulled open wide to the living room she could see Dick doing the "fish" with Kim, rubbing against her, and laughing. He was so much taller than Kim that Carrie was sure she was probably being strangled to death with his privates. Serves her right for allowing it, she decided.

The door chimes rang again and more people came into the room with loud, raucous laughter and four-letter words eliminating any need for adjectives at all. The "few couples" turned out to be at least ten and soon the den and living room were a sea of filled ashtrays, half-empty glasses, and layers of cigarette smoke hovering over them like so many flying carpets. Paul had had enough to drink by then so that he danced with Carrie. "Need a few to loosen up," as he was fond of saying. But he was a dependable dancer and though he certainly couldn't cha-cha much less "fish" he never missed the beat and gave a presentable appearance on the dance floor.

Some lethal looking female cut in on them and took Paul away from her for a dance, and Carrie couldn't help remembering Paul's old threat of getting his sex elsewhere. But she didn't think the gal would be his type. Carrie smiled, and made her way toward the kitchen to see if there was anything to eat since the catered buffet was nowhere in sight. It was a little past midnight and she was famished. She found some man she'd evidently missed before stooped in front of the open refrigerator. He was swaying a little and she wasn't sure if he was looking for food or ice. Rather than have to make polite conversation she ducked out again and waited to see if he'd leave. But some husband was making his way to her, to ask her to dance she was sure, so she skirted around the dancing couples to avoid him. When she'd made the full circle she slipped back into the kitchen and stopped dead in her tracks. The drunk who'd been there earlier was pushing himself against Kim, pinioning her against the sink and lewdly pumping his pelvis against her while his wet mouth ran over her shoulders and neck, down to the soft white flesh of her breasts. Kim saw her come in and gave her a shrug and a wink as if to say "Let the bastard have his kicks." Carrie felt sick, violently sick, and could feel her face pull into an ugly sneer at the scene. She wanted to throw up; that or slap Kim hard—either one. But instead she withdrew and headed for the sliding garden doors. She had to get some fresh air and get away from all those insane people.

The night air felt good, refreshing, as she stepped out and closed the door behind her. What in the world possessed Kim, she wondered. This wasn't the crazy Kim she knew, or was it? She'd never seen Kim with other people, now that she thought about it, much less at a party drinking and, and. . . . She wouldn't think about it, it was too disgusting.

"Cigarette?"

Carrie turned and made out George's outline as he came toward her from the yard, a small dot of red announcing his path. Suddenly she felt fear, a panic that George might be able to see into the kitchen, see Kim with that, that *thing*. Whatever stupidity Kim's drunken state might lead her to, Carrie didn't want her to get caught at it. "Why, yes, thank you, George," she said taking one from his extended pack and walking slowly away from the kitchen. "Quite a party," she added for lack of something better to say.

"I don't enjoy them," he said in a confidential tone, "as you can see." His finger pointed to the ground indicating that they were outside instead of inside.

"Why do you have them, then," Carrie asked.

"Oh," he said with a martyred sigh, "they're good for business. And, too, it gives Kim a chance to show her stuff. She loves parties."

"Does she?" Carrie said and tried to keep the picture of Kim in the kitchen out of her mind. "She never mentioned it. She doesn't really strike me as the type," she added.

He laughed cruelly. "You don't know her very well, do you. Let's see," he said and twisted his watch toward the light from the living room, "by now she should be in the kitchen, or maybe the bathroom, letting some poor guy with a hard-on get his feelies. It might be just a little too early yet, but soon."

His easy, conversational tone shocked Carrie more than the fact that he should know about Kim's antics. "You don't seem very concerned about it," she said slowly. It felt very odd that she should feel the cuckold while talking to the real one. After all, she wasn't Kim's husband. . . .

"I'm used to it," George said quietly. "And, after all, she's young."

"Tell me, George, do you love Kim?" It was a terribly rude question and she was more surprised than he to hear herself.

"That's a rhetorical question, Carrie," He paused while he lit another cigarette from his old one. "Love. Yes, well, I suppose you could call it love. I wouldn't marry anyone else, if that's what you mean. But then," he laughed, "if I had it to do over again I wouldn't get married at all."

"How long have you been married," she said.

"Four years, a little more."

Carrie hadn't realized Kim had been married for so long, but then too, there had never been any particular reason to mention it. "Don't you like children?"

"No. Should I?"

"There's no law about it." Carrie said a little stiffly.

"You're beginning to sound like Kim. Don't. . . ."

Carrie found herself becoming very annoyed with Greoge Willis. She glanced at him evenly, just a trace of a challenge in her hazel eyes. "Don't *what.*"

"Don't let her spoil you, Carrie. You're too lovely, entirely too lovely." He threw his cigarette into the night, then slowly put his arms around her waist drawing her to him so that her firm breasts pressed against his chest. "And you're too lovely to waste yourself. C'mon, relax, don't be afraid, I wouldn't hurt you. . . ."

She was too surprised to stop him and, she had to admit, even curious as to what Kim's husband was really like. Carrie let him kiss her but didn't help him at all. She just stood like a statue and let him have his kiss.

He kept his hands on her arms afterwards and smiled. "A little cooperation might have been in order, but that's all right. I like resistance."

"Get your filthy hands off of me," she ordered calmly.

He dropped his hands to his side and made a mock bow. "My time will come, I'm in no hurry."

It was too much for one evening, entirely too much, Carrie realized. She suddenly hated everyone, everyone at that party, Kim, George, all of them. Couldn't they ever think about anything else? She stood for a moment so that George wouldn't think she'd been afraid, then turned and entered the house to find Paul and go home. She wanted to go home where she was safe.

She found him and disentangled a happy, smiling, dancing Paul from some suburban wench and steered him out the door and into the car. Carrie drove them home and helped him into bed where he immediately fell into a sound sleep, his mouth open just a little with a light snore catching in his throat. She sat next to him in the bed and unable to sleep lit a cigarette. She wondered if Paul had taken that female's phone number, or if he had kissed her while they danced. His business trips, for instance. How much of it was really business? What did he do when he went out to dinner, and the hours afterwards? There were always women hanging around in hotels and bars. Somehow, though, the idea of his playing around while on a business trip didn't bother her too much. It was "out there" and had nothing to do with her. But his drooling over that woman wasn't the thing that had really disturbed her either, and she knew it.

Really, she thought recreating the party, it was the most disgusting display I've ever seen in my life. The worst was that Kim should allow, that Kim should invite, that . . . and it was then that for the first time in eleven years Carrie recognized what was going on inside of her, remembered the anguish and torment of a kind of love she'd never had with Paul or any other man. It was then that Carrie knew she was falling in love with Kim . . . if it hadn't already happened, if it wasn't too late.

Chapter VI

Paul's flight left La Guardia at 12:45 that Saturday afternoon and it had been difficult to get him organized enough to move quickly; as usual after a party, he was both groggy and grumpy and kept saying that he thought he'd put it off until Sunday—there was another flight and after all there wasn't much he could do on Saturday. But Carrie kept reminding him that he'd been invited to Sunday dinner by a very good account and he didn't want to arrive there all tired or risk a delayed flight. She'd have said anything to get him out of the house so she could think! On top of everything else on her mind, she'd had a pretty stiff shock that morning. While packing his suit, the new one, she'd found his address book and other papers in his inside pocket. With nothing particular in mind she had leafed through the book. She was more than just a little startled to see under *Chicago* a list of three or four women's names. Just first names; Paul was discreet. But there they were, neat little handwritten letters that would damn him in any divorce court, she knew. Under the I's there was Indianapolis and its set of names; the B's had Boston; and it seemed unreal to Carrie that Paul could really be having such an active secret life. Something would show through in their relationship, wouldn't it? She hated Paul. Hated him for humiliating her, for torturing her with his dirty little sex problems. Whores! she thought ruthlessly. Filthy creatures . . . and then he has the gall to make love to me too! But the stunning shock came under the N's: New York! It was too much to absorb. How many times must she have passed a woman he'd taken to bed. She felt totally numbed by this discovery; unable to even let it settle upon her mind. *I should have guessed,* she thought.

What was it he had said? That she didn't understand? Well, she understood now all right! She understood that he was no different from any other man—they only thought about one thing. Show her a man and she'd show you a skull filled with semen . . . that's all any man is, she now swore under her breath. Carrie also remembered her own threat so long ago, that she would leave him. But it *was* so long ago. What she could have, might have, done ten years before couldn't be taken so lightly now. Now there were two children, a home, a lifetime shared, bonds of common experience . . . how could she leave Paul without destroying her own life and that of the children? And it was strange how she was unable to feel jealousy about it; it was closer to hurt, to betrayal. Well, he'd warned her—she couldn't say he hadn't. But she'd been unable to believe it . . . until last night, until now. He just wasn't the type, she would've sworn to that. She had felt weak and sick. Carrie wanted him to leave on his trip, to get him out of the way so she could think about it more carefully. She didn't have the strength yet to confront him with it; she didn't really know how she felt about it yet.

And this discovery, coupled with her feelings of turmoil about Kim the night before, left her completely in a fog. It was too much at one time for anyone to contend with . . . something had to give. She wanted to be alone.

Both the kids wanted to go with them to the airport so it was a hectic ride down the Hutchinson River Parkway— safely prohibiting Carrie from saying anything to Paul— and over the Bronx Whitestone Bridge. There were minor squabbles about one of them taking up too much room in the back seat, even in Paul's larger Nash Ambassador, then Sara wanted to sit up front and Carrie couldn't allow that without Sambo putting up an argument, and Paul kept telling them to sit still and be quiet and when they reached the toll he didn't have the exact change—and so it went. Sambo wanted to know when he'd be old enough to be a pilot, and had Paul ever flown a plane, and then needled Sara by télling her she could never be a pilot no matter what. Sara, having not even the vaguest idea of what a pilot was, simply argued that she had more toys than Sambo did anyway.

At long last, Paul was walking up the ramp to his flight; they waved him off, and Carrie was finally driving back home. The kids were strangely silent for the most part. Once Sara wanted to know if that's what happened to people when they died, did they just get on a airplane and never come back but stay in the clouds. Carrie didn't feel like discussing death at that moment and gave a rather abrupt "No," with which the kids were wise enough not to argue. Carrie suddenly wondered if Paul intended to be on the make for Kim. No. He couldn't be. That would be too stupid, too low—but the image made her furious! Carrie needed some time to herself, probably a lot of time, to put her thoughts in order and come to some kind of conclusion about her feelings toward Kim. Eleven years was a lot of lifetime to've gone by without ever having the old pull toward gay life; she was a very different woman from that easy-going, devil-may-care girl with the short hair and the thumbs always in the slacks pockets. She had worn a dress only to go to work, and since she wasn't really a bull-dyke type she never had any trouble "passing." But otherwise, it was tight-fitting pants and a tailored shirt fresh from the Chinese laundry, sneakers, and a blazer if she went out. Out. Gay bars crowed with obnoxious creatures, human but neither men nor women, whose sole purpose was to get drunk and/or—preferably *and*—find a girl friend for the evening, for a week, for as long at it lasted. Carrie had not liked that kind of thing and had always pretty much stayed away from gay bars; she didn't see why she should have to be downright promiscuous just because she was gay. But she always had a lot of gay friends, couples who'd been together a year or more and held responsible jobs and were comfortably settled with each other—until it broke up. She stayed far, far away from the dykes. They were just as grotesque to her as they were to the straight world around her. She wanted to be able to go to the movies with friends dressed in slacks and not be hyperconscious of whether people were whispering about them or not. If she was gay, okay, she was gay but she didn't see any advantage to being a card-carrying lesbian. What for? To ask for even more trouble than that kind of life handed out to begin with? Not for her. And through these friends who "passed" she met other girls, girls with some ambition in life besides sexual conquest—in their own way they were really much worse than the most lecherous of men—and in the course of a little more than six years she had had three lovers and two blind-drunk, one-night affairs.

It was with sincere relief that she pulled the Nash into the garage and let the kids scramble out ahead of her. She opened the back door, gave them a no-nonsense command to change into their playclothes and hang up their good clothes, and put on some water for coffee. It seemed like only seconds later that they both came thumping downstairs and, grabbing some fruit, ran out the door to play. She just knew they hadn't hung up their clothes and that everything would be an inside-out wad lying on the floor, but she didn't have the energy to enforce her order at that point. She had to think and she just didn't want to. Her life had been so quiet, so nice and safe, and then Kim had to come along. Maybe if she didn't think about it it would go away, she thought, but knew better. Well, what is there to think *about,* she asked herself. There's nothing I can do about it except to not see Kim anymore. Period. She couldn't amputate the gay part of her brain, could she? But Carrie wished to God that one could. How much easier it would be! She would not, could not, jeopardize her present life—more for the children than anything else. She supposed that she probably still loved Paul, despite everything. It wasn't something you turned off and on again. But it was a love based on duration, wearing well, knowing her subject so thoroughly that it never presented any major problems . . . or hadn't, anyway, until that morning. This new situation, well, she'd have to think about that separately; one problem at a time was already one problem too many.

As for herself, right then she just didn't know; she simply couldn't force herself to ask what it was she really wanted. She knew that there was no question about the children; they were all that really mattered to her. And she did want the security of married life, but she also wanted the feeling of elation and excitement that came with really being in love. And that, she knew, she would never know with any man! Even though—provided it wasn't too often —she'd grown to rather enjoy copulation with Paul, she could never achieve an orgasm with him. Maybe there was something physically wrong with her, though she strongly doubted it. So many women, according to medical articles, were incapable of orgasm. But the problem went deeper than that with Carrie; she could achieve it with a woman! Could, and did, and often found herself nearly insatiable.

"Oh, Paul," she whispered to herself, "I *do* know what you went through . . . I just couldn't do anything about it!" All the old memories that had been so long out of her mind, so buried and forgotten that they no longer bothered her as they had those first couple of years with Paul, came rushing back. But now there was Kim.

"No!" she said. She would not, definitely not allow Kim or any other woman to ruin her life now. Perhaps Paul had solved his problem in his own way, had given in to infidelity, but that didn't mean she could do the same thing. It would crucify all that their home meant to her. But then, she had to admit, there didn't seem to be much of a decision involved actually—Kim was not gay.

Carrie picked up the steaming kettle as if it were the root of all her trouble, and poured the boiling water into the cup with its brown, powdered coffee, then stood for a second just staring out the kitchen window at all the yards of the homes on her block; the homes that housed normal poeple with normal lives and normal desires. *It wasn't fair!* Why did there have to be straight people and gay people? She hadn't asked for it; why did it have to happen to her? There'd never been any major traumas in her childhood; no man had ever raped her; she'd never seen her parents in bed; no evil older woman had perverted her as a child; she'd never even had a crush on a teacher! Nothing at all. She'd played with dolls, swooned over Frank Sinatra like all the other girls in school, and there had been a couple of boys she'd liked better than the others even though they never asked her for a date. Did God decide these things? Not if everything she'd read on the subject were true; and she had every reason to think they were true. It'd be as foolish to blame God for it as it would be to blame Him for handing out freckles and red hair, or for the fact that there were drunks and criminals in the world. Why blame Him for what science had proven to be genetics and environmental maladjustment, neuroses and psychoses? Like so many other things in life, there just didn't seem to be any obvious reason—sometimes they just were.

A perfectly average life until her senior year in high school when Carrie'd fallen completely in love with a new girl in school. Just like that. She had followed the girl around for many days and finally had had the nerve to ask if she could sit at her table at the school cafeteria. Carrie could still remember the smell of vegetable soup, so pleasantly pungent, and the ever present meat loaf with brown gravy over the heavy white scoop of potatoes. It had been a rainy day, so that added to the usual odors of the cafeteria was the smell of damp coats and musty umbrellas and the heavy smell of manufactured rubber boots.

"Sure, sit down," the girl had answered idly.

Carrie removed her dishes from the tray and placed them on the small space left opposite the new girl. She sat down quietly and played with her food. "I saw you in Civics yesterday."

"Are we in the same class?" the girl asked with forced politeness.

"Yes. Gym and English too." She pushed her mashed potatoes around through the gravy, not daring to look at the girl. "Your name's Martha . . . mine's Carrie."

"I hadn't noticed you in class."

"Oh." Carrie laughed nervously. "Well, I'm there all right."

Martha stared at her for a moment. "I suppose so." She turned away and looked casually at the other students in the cafeteria, then back to Carrie. "I suppose you want to be friends?"

Carrie was unsure of what to say. "Well," she laughed again, "I guess if you don't have any yet you could do worse than start with me." She felt painfully thin and angular next to Martha's healthy rounded body.

"I suppose you're terribly bright, or something."

"No. Usually *B*s . . . unless it's something I really enjoy, like history."

"History! That dreadful waste of time? Well," Martha smiled warmly, "I suppose you might make a good friend after all . . . I always need help with my homework in history. Wish we didn't have to take it. Who cares about all those dead people and the past? I want to know about today."

"I like it," Carrie said in almost a whisper. She didn't want Martha to think she was some kind of freak or anything. Since their next class was English the two girls left together toward the east wing of the dark, ugly building with its barred windows and factory-like atmosphere.

As the weeks went by Carrie found herself constantly over at Martha's house helping her with her homework, or just listening to Martha's huge collection of popular records. Martha was never in the same mood twice; one day she'd seem genuinely glad to see Carrie and the next ignore her and the next be annoyed with her because Carrie hadn't completed her homework for her. Carrie sensed that she was being primed to write Martha's term papers for her, but didn't care as long as she could be near her. But something started to go wrong when Martha went out on a date with one of the Varsity stars. She lost all interest in Carrie, or school, or anything else. Carrie was no longer asked to come over because Martha would stay after school to watch the team practice. Carrie tried to impress upon Martha that she would flunk out at the rate Martha was ignoring her classes, but Martha wouldn't listen. Without fully knowing why, Carrie was totally crushed by Martha's indifference. She had never expected to be loved by Martha, but she hadn't expected to be ignored either. It wasn't as if she made any demands upon Martha; in fact, if anything it had been the other way around.

Then the final hurt came when her school counselor had called Carrie in for a chat and in very embarrassed, hushed tones explained that she understood how some girls developed "crushes" while in their teens, but that, well, the world took a dim view of such things and often gave it dirty names like "queer" and "homosexual." Carrie was humiliated. She'd never even thought in those terms, in anything physical. She'd never even touched Martha—though she had often wanted to.

Actually, as Carrie looked back on it and her counselor now, the old dyke—as she clearly had been, Carrie since realized—had put her on the road to homosexuality. If what she had felt for Martha was "queer" and it was considered not nice, then she intended to find out more about it and just what it was and why! And what a wealth of source material she found in New York City where she soon discovered the bars and congregating places. She turned eighteen just before graduation and immediately afterwards moved to Manhattan and found a job. Naturally, her parents had disapproved strenuously about it, but there had been no dissuading her.

Unexpectedly, the telephone rang and Carrie jumped in

71

surprise, brought harshly back to the present. She walked over to it and picked up the receiver. "Hello?"

"How's your head? Mine's like a gourd." Kim laughed.

The last person in the world Carrie wanted to talk to right then, but also, she had to admit, the first. She wanted to hang up, to cry, to reach out and hold Kim, to . . . to just *something!* She felt as if her world were collapsing around her and she had nowhere to turn. But then she remembered the scene of Kim in the kitchen with that creep and felt a chill of anger crawl over her flesh. "I don't think I had as much as you," she answered coolly.

"You busy right now?"

"What did you have in mind," Carrie asked.

"Brr," Kim said with a light giggle, "you're either awful guilty or awful mad. I'll be right over."

Carrie's immediate thought was to tell her not to, but then decided that Kim may as well come by. Give her a chance to take a long, hard look at both Kim and herself. Perhaps all she really felt for Kim was a crush of sorts, some left-field maternal instinct or something. It was odd, though, that Kim was volunteering to come to her house; it was the first time. But Kim's next question answered that.

"Paul off on his trip yet? George is lying around in his undershorts trying to look sexy and I think it's disgusting the way men with hairy stomachs can lie around the house like that."

"Yes, Paul's on his way."

"Great. We'll dish about the party. See you in a second."

Kim hung up and Carrie replaced the receiver and stood still for a moment. "Dish about the party," she sneered. An old gay term the "straights" took over, why that had been popular in her day! Yes. It was a good idea for Kim to come over then, in the harsh light of day and being completely objective about the entire situation. She'd no sooner put the kettle on again, and washed up the breakfast dishes she'd not had time to do before Paul's flight, than she heard Kim's Ford drive up the gravel driveway outside the kitchen. She was wearing the same outfit, dungarees and haltar, that Carrie had met her in; and that seemed appropriate.

The backdoor opened slightly and Kim's voice called loudly, "Carrie? I'm here. . . ."

"I'm right here, Kim. C'mon in." She couldn't help noticing that Kim didn't show any signs of drinking from the party; in fact, she looked refreshed and youthful and full of spirit.

"Hi," Kim said walking in and throwing herself onto the padded chrome chair in front of the chrome and Formica table. "Boy, am I bushed. What're you looking so glum about? You and Paul have a fight? Saw him with Alice last night . . . quite a boy, your husband," she snickered.

Carrie could just imagine what Paul might have been doing. Carrie never begrudged a man a tasteful, drunken drool or two over a nice looking woman, but she couldn't be sure of Paul anymore. She could not know what he was up to—or with whom. "No, we didn't have a fight."

"Well, then," Kim sat up with a sly expression on her face. "What were *you* up to then, hmm?"

"I was in the garden necking with your husband!" Carrie said before she knew it, but realized that it was probably only because she wanted to hurt Kim, shock her, even as Kim had hurt her.

"Isn't that George too much?" Kim laughed. "Swears he's Zachary Scott. Enjoy it?" She reached over and inspected the salt shaker, unperturbed.

"Not particularly. I found him rather awkward." If anything will get a woman, Carrie reasoned, it's having another woman put down her husband's screwing abilities; it makes her feel that she's missing something.

"George? Awkward?" Kim just stared at her for a moment then shrugged. "Guess you really put him in a bag then. I've never known him to be awkward. . . ." Her eyebrows came together in a serious, thoughtful expression and Carrie was glad that she'd hit home. Something had to penetrate that girl's facade. Carrie didn't make any comment but just let Kim stew.

73

A few silent seconds went by before Carrie lifted the kettle in silent questioning. "Nah," Kim said, "I don't want coffee." She looked briefly around the kitchen. "Got anything to drink? Something to pick me up a little?"

"I don't know," Carrie answered, and had to agree that it sounded like a good idea. She could use a stiff drink right then. "Let me go look in Paul's stock."

Kim laughed as she went through the dining room. *"Paul's* stock," she teased. "Hey, girl, what year you livin' in? Haven't you any rights?"

Carrie didn't bother to answer what was on her tongue, that Paul was twice the man George would ever think of being—whether he was faithful or not—and in their house he ran the roost, as it *should* be. But suddenly she felt like Mr. Arnold, the personnel manager, and felt guilty toward Kim. She found about half a bottle of dry vermouth and a full fifth of unopened gin. She couldn't help an involuntary hesitation before removing the bottle; Paul might notice and object. But Kim's remark about her rights ended any indecision and she took out the two bottles and closed the cupboard door like a sneak-thief, as if Paul were hiding behind the curtains spying on her.

"I just was thinking that I've never been in your house," Kim said. She'd pulled out another chair and had her feet propped up.

"Feel like seeing the rest?" Carrie asked. "It's not particularly impressive."

"Later," Kim yawned. "Let's have a drink first. Where're your kids? Never met them either."

"Out. They waltz in and out pretty much as they please till supper time."

"Oh." She didn't seem very interested in pursuing the subject. She stared at her feet for a minute, sighed, then stood up and crossed over to the sink where Carrie was standing. "What's taking you so long," she asked just as Carrie poured the drinks. "That's more like it," she said and took a long swallow. Her eyes were closed and, Carrie thought, if one didn't know better one might think she was taking mother's milk. She sipped on hers and made a small face. She didn't make them nearly as well as Kim, they tasted a little bit like perfume.

"Too much vermouth," Kim said and poured more gin into the decanter. "There. That should do it." She tasted it again and nodded. "Pour yours back in and I'll fix it right."

Carrie did as she was told and moved over to the table and sat down. She felt numb, completely numb. Her tongue seemed swollen and leaden and her arms leaned heavily on the table top. A feeling of defeat, complete and utter defeat; she just didn't have the strength anymore to battle with herself, Paul or with Kim, or even to be the demure wife and busy mother. She just wanted to lie down somewhere and never wake up, never have to face life or decisions or problems. Just sleep, peaceful sleep.

"Whatcha thinking," Kim asked softly sitting down opposite her. "You look like you're miles away."

"I was," Carrie answered tiredly. "I was in lollipop land," she added, then smiled to herself at her fantasies. It seemed strange to be able to smile.

"You feel that way today too?" Kim asked. "I got up this morning with the most awful sensation of 'What for?' You know what I mean? Another party, another day, but the same people, the same George, the same empty life. You at least have your family, I suppose that helps . . . makes you feel needed and worthwhile. Me? I haven't got anything except a cute face and a decent figure and I'll be losing both of those in a few years."

Carrie finished off her drink and poured them each some more. She knew she shouldn't have another because they were strong and she was feeling the punch already, but she could always take a nap and sleep them off. "Why don't you have children then?" she suddenly asked Kim.

Kim gave an evil laugh. "I can't. Didn't you know that? Thought that'd be the first thing George would tell you; he tells everyone else. No heir for the Georgie, doesn't that just grab you?"

Carrie shook her head in reply and suddenly felt terribly compassionate toward Kim. She was such a baby. "Why don't you adopt a child," she said.

Kim shrugged. "Who cares anyway? Can you see me pinning diapers?"

"You know, Kim," Carrie said slowly, "you do one helluva lot of shrugging. Why don't you just shoot yourself!"

Kim's mouth fell open and she gawked at Carrie. "What are you talking about," she said after a moment.

"I'm talking about your big fat mouth and your constantly hunched shoulders, *that's* what I'm talking about!" All her anger from the night before, with Paul and Kim both, came rushing to the front, anger and scorn at Kim who had everything with no major problems other than child bearing, which she could get around—she had the money—and she was tired of Kim's constant complaining about nothing, never taking anything seriously. "Everytime you open your mouth you're making fun of what most people hold very sacred in life. What's the matter Kim, can't you take life? Can't you face it?"

"Huh?"

"And then comes the sweet-young-thing routine, the little girl who's just so mixed up that she says naughty things and comes apologizing. Grow up, Kim, just plain grow up!"

"What in the hell's gotten into you," Kim demanded but with an almost frightened smile. "I've seen hangovers in my day . . ."

"I'm not hungover, Kim. Just tired of your constant prattle about nothing, and putting down of everything serious. Why don't you admit you'd love to have kids, and you'd like to be able to be in love with your husband and move out of suburbia with its noontime cocktails and have a decent home somewhere and lead a decent life for a change instead of that empty-headed vacuum you exist in. . . ." She paused and only then realized that Kim was crying, the tears slowly running down her cheeks. Carrie felt terrible. She'd had no right to say those things, no right at all. She knew most of it had come from the discovery of

Paul's cheating and she was taking it out on Kim. But then, Kim rushed over to her and, kneeling down on the floor, rested her head in Carrie's lap. She just stayed there until Carrie, unable to forgive herself, stroked the younger girl's hair and face. "I'm sorry, Kim. Really."

Kim's head came up and she wiped her eyes with hands that trembled slightly. "You some kind of an iconoclast?" she asked with a feeble smile.

Carrie smiled back. "I guess so," she said. "I . . . I was pretty upset last night and this morning. Guess I had to take it out on someone and picked you. Forgive me?"

Kim arose slowly and, her eyes all dry then, giggled nervously. "Remind me to stay away the next time, will you?" She poured them a third drink and raised her glass to Carrie's. "But you're right, of course. I do talk too much, put down everything. I don't know why, Carrie, honest. Things just come out of my mouth. Lots of times I'm sorry even while I'm saying them but by then it's too late. I don't know why, I just don't."

"Let's forget about it, shall we?" Carrie said guiltily.

"All right," Kim agreed and stood up to make another batch of drinks.

Carrie thought to tell her not to, that she had gotten plenty high already, but decided that after her cruel display she couldn't deprive Kim of a few drinks. She'd buy some more gin later on, at a different store from their regular one. And with that decision she decided to kill the bottle, to get nicely tanked.

Kim returned to the table and put the decanter down. "What were you upset about," she asked quietly.

"Nothing," Carrie mumbled.

"C'mon. If I had to take the brunt of it the least you could do is tell me what brought it all on."

Carrie's mind was a little muddled with the alcohol but not so much that she didn't know what she was saying. It was more that she ceased to care. And she needed to talk to someone about it, if only to hear her own thoughts articulated. Eleven years of bottling up had to go some-where; things covered up for so long might rot but they didn't evaporate. She'd pulled the cork last night; now it was time to find out what the genie would do.

"Tell me, Kim," she began, then paused.

"Go on."

Carrie glanced at her and held her eyes. "Do you care if George plays around? I mean, really care?"

"Is that it? Paul's having a little hanky-panky?" Kim laughed coarsely. "Tell him to fuck off . . . don't let him get you."

Carrie nodded as if she'd really expected Kim to say something like that. "You're young and childless . . . I'm not. I've got a lot of years and emotions tied up in this marriage."

"Well, whenever I'm sure that George's playing—more than just a one-night stand, that is—I see to it that I have an affair too. Men are stupid, really. Two-legged dogs in the manger. The moment they think that someone else is getting what they left home to cheat on, then they come running back! Now that you mention it, though, George has been out a good deal more lately. I wonder if he's up to something redheaded. . . ."

"How come you don't divorce George? I mean, if you can cheat on him too you certainly can't love him very much. What holds you to him? You could remarry. . . ." She took another swallow from her drink and realized she was beginning to get drunk.

"Don't be naive . . . what for? He pays the bills, I get just about anything I want from him. He's not perfect, but I'm not a brass ring either." Kim leaned forward and rested her hand on Carrie's. "Don't let it bug you. All men stray once in awhile. They can't help it."

Carrie had to smile to herself. It wasn't Paul who couldn't help it . . . it was herself. She'd pushed him into straying—he hadn't wanted to. Well, she'd brought it on herself but she didn't think it would be proper to mention to Kim why. But she had to mention it. She had to tell somebody. The whole situation between Kim, and Paul, was proving more than she could handle in martyred silence. She raised her glass and stared into it myopically.

78

"I can't blame Paul," she heard herself say as if she were a silent onlooker, "I forced him into it."

Kim's eyebrows raised quizzically but she said nothing.

"Just for curiosity's sake," Carrie said slowly, "have you ever noticed anything at all, well, unusual about me? As a person, I mean?"

"Unusual?" Kim sat down looking like Sara when she was confronted with a question she didn't understand.

"Strange, let's say. Different." Carrie's tongue wasn't thick yet, but her eyes certainly felt peculiar. All those martinis in the early afternoon . . . and there she sat with another in front of her. Well, she'd gone that far . . . it was impossible to not go on.

"No," Kim answered. "Can't say I have. You're just you. Of course," she smiled sheepishly, "I'll admit I'm maybe a little too selfish to notice much in other people."

"Well," Carrie said sitting back with, oddly enough, a smug sensation. "There is. Didn't I ever tell you? I thought sure Paul would . . . except he doesn't know."

"Stop mimicking me," Kim commanded softly. "What are you talking about."

"My big secret," Carrie answered and waved her arm as if the entire world knew about it. "You know why I married Paul?"

Kim didn't say anything, but finished off her drink and poured more.

"Because he was the first man who asked me to marry him. In fact, if you must know," she became very confidential, "he was my first man, period. Whatd'ya think of that!"

"You're getting drunk," Kim said but Carrie wasn't sure which of them she was referring to.

"I'd been a lesbian for years," Carrie continued. "A lesbian for the FBI," she added, and laughed loudly at her own joke.

"You?" Kim asked incredulously.

"Little ol' me."

Kim whistled lightly through her teeth. "I'll be goddamned. Miss Holy Family a friggin' lesbian!" She fell back against her chair and roared with laughter.

Carrie became very serious. "You don't care? It doesn't shock you?"

"Why the hell should it? What the hell do I care what you were or did before . . . or even now, for that matter. A *lesbian!*" She laughed then made kissing noises at Carrie. "And necking with George, of all people. . . ."

"Don't change the subject. I should think you'd have a little more consideration for my past. It's cost me dearly, I'll tell you."

"I met a lesbian once,". Kim said. "But she was all ugly 'n fat 'n had a man's haircut. You got any pictures of you when you were a fag?"

"Women aren't fags, men are. And no, I burned all those old pictures when I married Paul."

"You mean he doesn't know?" Kim asked with all trace of humor gone. "You never told him?"

"Never. You've met him. Do you think he'd of married me if he'd known?"

"No," Kim said thoughtfully. "No, I don't suppose he would."

"You're damn right. And, anyway, that's what started his playing around. Not directly, but, well, he thinks I'm pretty cold, y'know."

"Do you still prefer girls? Does he suspect now?" Kim lost all interest in Paul's affairs with this juicier news.

"No, y'nut. That's not it. I mean that after eleven years of a nice, simple quiet life I find out he's running around . . . and then . . . I've got to meet you and get all loused up again."

"What've I got to do with anything," Kim asked sincerely.

"That's just it, y'nut, what I've been trying to tell you. Something about last night brought it all back to me. Finding out about Paul, or maybe it was you necking in the kitchen, or George even . . . I don't know. But all the old feelings came back, the loneliness and heartache. After eleven years. . . ."

"Jeez, Carrie. . . ."

"Yeh, 'Jeez Carrie.' Anyway, I decided you weren't good for me, I decided this morning that I wasn't going to see you anymore."

"But you're not falling for me, are you? I mean, well, I like you Carrie, even love you, but . . . well, I'm just not cut out for that sort of thing. You know what I mean?"

"How can I know what you mean when I am cut out for that sort of thing!"

"Oh. Well, but you're not, are you?"

"In love with you?" Carrie put her head back for a second and squinted at Kim but her brain began to feel like the last pickle in the jar so she put her head back down again. "I don't know. I don't think so, anyway. I just don't know."

Kim reached over for the cigarettes and lit one for each of them. "Well, let me tell you something, Carrie Anderson of the great family-that-stays-together-kick, you're not. I probably represent the old times to you, being on your own and doing as you damn well pleased. Paul may be a nice guy and all that, but really, Carrie, he's more like your father than your husband. He's pompous and not overly bright, and if he's screwing around too . . ."

"Paul's very bright. Look at the agency," Carrie argued.

"No, I mean bright in personality. You know, fun and good laughs." Kim leaned forward unexpectedly and placed a very soft and dry kiss on Carrie's lips, then sat back. "There. Did that do anything to you? Feel any tingles 'n things?" She had a small smile on her face but it was a tender one.

Carrie blinked a couple of times. "No. Not a thing." And it was true, too. She'd not felt anything more than she would if one of the kids had kissed her.

"There. Y'see? You're not in love with me. You just had to talk to someone, get it out of you."

Carrie smiled in nodding agreement and felt a tremendous relief. Mostly, she supposed in somewhat of a fog, because she wouldn't have to give up her friendship with Kim. She'd been beastly to Kim and she wanted to make

81

it up. They finished up all the martinis and somehow the talk easily drifted to the party again and although Carrie still didn't like the picture of Kim with that creep it didn't bother her as much as it had.

A little past three, Kim stood up unsteadily to go home. She placed her arm around Carrie's shoulder at the door and gave her a reassuring hug. It felt very odd to Carrie to have a warm, woman's breast against her own arm, but nothing to worry about. In fact, she had even gained a true friend, someone who knew all about her and didn't care, wasn't repelled. She closed the door after Kim and dragged herself upstairs and flopped across the big bed for a much-needed nap. She didn't hear a thing until almost past five o'clock when Sara woke her to tell her she was hungry.

Chapter VII

Late Saturday night Carrie went to bed a very confused woman. She knew she'd told Kim about her past, and for the most part could reconstruct their conversation, but still something nagged at her. Perhaps it was just that in her inebriated state she'd not been able to clearly read any hidden reactions or secret expressions in Kim's eyes. Or had she perhaps forgotten some important gesture or word . . . she couldn't remember and it plagued her to have been so stupid as to confess everything when she wasn't in complete control. But then, it was the first time she'd ever "confessed" so a certain leeway had to be granted, and anyway, she was quite sure that Kim had not objected in the least—she'd kissed her, hadn't she? To be sure, a token kiss, an experimental one more for Carrie's benefit than Kim's, but still. . . .

She'd fallen asleep fitfully and the unusually hot October night didn't help matters any. There wasn't a breeze anywhere and the air was thick with humidity so that she was terribly conscious of every breath she took. If she hadn't had a hangover that morning, she certainly had one then. She would really have to cut down on this martini business once and for all. After all, even Paul was beginning to notice it, make casual remarks, and she didn't want any more trouble about anything. She'd dozed off with that thought, and finally fell into a deeper sleep and began to dream of having an affair with George who was sometimes George and sometimes a faceless woman she seemed to know but couldn't recognize. There was a bell that kept ringing somewhere, almost like school class change bells and in that semi-conscious state while dreaming she recognized the girl as the girl she'd first loved in high school and felt herself smile. It wasn't quite right, she wasn't really the same girl, but it was enough of an identification to allow the sequence of the dream to continue . . . except for that damn bell. . . .

She awoke abruptly to the sound of the telephone next to the bed, fumbled a moment muttering to her self, and picked it up. "Hello," she demanded.

A vaguely familiar, hoarse man's voice replied. "Carrie? Honey?"

"Paul?" she asked back.

"I'm sorry to wake you up like this, hon. I'm at the airport. I don't feel so hot. . . ."

"Which airport, Paul?" she said wide awake then, forgetting everything but his illness. Paul had only been sick once in their entire married life and it had only been a cold, just enough to keep him in bed for a couple of days but nothing really serious.

"La Guardia," he answered but his breath came in short gasps. "At the ticket counter . . . I've got to sit down, hon, I don't think I can stand up much longer. . . ."

"I'll be right there, Paul. Ask if they've got a doctor there but don't go anywhere without telling the airline where'll you'll be. Have you got that, Paul? Paul?"

"Yeah, yeah I've got it. Hurry up, will you? And Carrie," he added slowly, "I'm sorry to get you up like this."

"Never mind that. Go sit down. I'll be there fast as I can."

They both hung up and she quickly turned on the light and threw on a pair of slacks and a blouse, passed a brush through her hair and went into Sambo's room softly. "Sambo, wake up, honey."

His dark, short hair stood in tufts over his head as he opened his eyes groggily. "What?"

"Sambo, I've got to go get Daddy. He's at the airport and not feeling well. Sambo! Wake up."

"Sure, Mom. Dad's not feeling well."

"Now listen, I won't be gone long but I want you to get up and go sleep in Sara's room. C'mon, Sambo, get up now."

"Is it morning?" he asked swinging his legs over the side of the bed.

"No, darling, it's not. Now what did I just tell you?" She steered him out of his room and toward Sara's.

"You're going to get Dad at the airport," he yawned and shuffled down the hall, "and you won't be long and I'm to sleep in Sara's room."

"That's my boy," she said proudly. "If she wakes up while I'm gone, you take care of her, explain I'll be right back. Okay?"

"Sure, Mom. I'll take care of everything," he whispered and crawled into the twin bed in Sara's room. "Move over," he muttered and gave Sara a light shove. "I'll take care of everything . . ." he said as Carrie kissed him on the forehead and tiptoed out the door and ran down to the car. All the way to the airport she kept thinking what a regular trooper Sambo was and of how terribly pleased she was with him, how glad to be his mother.

* * * *

The harsh morning sun was kept out of the bedroom by the upturned Venetian blinds as the doctor straightened up from Paul's bedside. "Nothing too much to worry about," Dr. Clark said in the usual irritating tone of optimism only a doctor can have, "mild case of pneumonia.

At least," he laughed, "nothing to worry about in this day and age."

"Pneumonia!" Carrie gasped.

"Now, now, Mrs. Anderson. There's nothing to worry about. I gave him a shot of penicillin and I'll give you a couple of prescriptions to get filled. He'll be fit as a fiddle in no time." He ushered Carrie out of the room and closed the door quietly behind him. "Lots of rest, that's what he needs the most. Has he been under any major strain lately?"

"Nothing more than usual," she answered. "My husband is a very hard worker. He was going on a business trip, that is, he'd just arrived in Chicago and, well, I'm not too clear on just exactly what happened but he came right back yesterday, last night. . . ."

"Well, let's not worry about that. He's going to be fine," Dr. Clark said leading the way down the stairs to the front door. "I'll look in on him first thing tomorrow morning but you've got my number if you notice any change before then."

"What about food, if he wakes up I mean, he'll want. . . ."

"If he wakes up, which I strongly doubt, and is hungry, just give him some broth for now. Let's see how he is to-morrow."

They stood by the open door and Carrie was more than slightly aggravated by him; it was so obvious he was trying to get out as soon as possible. He knew he'd have midnight calls when he became a doctor; that was part of his job. Bad enough he'd not shown up until daybreak but that he should be so callous as not even to attempt to conceal his desire to get back to his golf game, or his breakfast, or whatever, when a patient of his lay upstairs with penu-monia. . . . Well! Paul might have died during the night for all he cared. But conditioned as she was to respect the medical profession and be grateful for any crumbs of ad-vice, she thanked him and waited until he drove off before closing the door and returning to their bedroom to see how Paul was.

Sambo crept into the room behind her. "How's Dad now?"

"Shh. He's much better. The doctor says he needs lots of rest so let's let him sleep. C'mon," she said quietly and they left the room. Sambo was still in his pajamas and barefooted. "Go put on your robe and your slippers," she told him once outside. "No point in having everyone sick in the house."

She went downstairs to the kitchen and started breakfast for herself and the children, and shortly thereafter Sambo came downstairs with Sara trailing behind in her little terrycloth robe and dark blue bunny slippers. "Daddy's gonna die?" she asked.

"No, of course not," Carrie answered and picked her up for a reassuring kiss. "Daddy's just not feeling well, like the time you were in bed right after Christmas. Remember?"

Sara nodded but not too surely. Carrie doubted if she did remember being sick; the blessings of childhood, she thought. She served them their breakfast and while they ate it explained to them that they were going to have to be very very especially good while Paul was sick. No arguments or running in the house, no ball playing near Paul's window, and especially to talk softly anytime they were near or in the house. She put Sambo on his Scout's honor and knew she'd just have to cope with Sara when the time came.

"Daddy's going in the airplane and never coming back?" Sara wanted to know.

"No, Daddy's staying in bed to get well. Now you two go on upstairs and get dressed . . . quietly, y'understand?" She'd never understand children's preoccupation with death but supposed she'd been the same way too. Except that her family had been very religious Methodists and it must have been easier for her mother to simply say that God took people to heaven. She couldn't remember now what her mother had said, and really didn't care at that moment. She had no desire to connect Paul with death. Then for the first time, she wondered what she *would* do if Paul died. Oh, not right then—she believed the doctor about that—but just in general in the next few years or so. Just what would she do? For a second, gay life crossed her mind, but not for any longer—Sambo and Sara would make such a thing quite impossible, even if she wanted to. But Carrie doubted that she would remarry. She'd never known any other man she could be so comfortable with. A job would become imperative. Paul had insurance to pay off the house if he died, and a little extra to pay up bills, but that was all. He didn't believe very much in insurance, always said that any woman fool enough to marry a man who can't leave enough behind to provide for his family deserves to be poor. She'd never thought about it at the time enough to argue the point. But now it struck her as a very pigheaded and spurious kind of logic. She didn't mind the thought of having to work, but why should the children be deprived of a college education, or why should they probably have to sell the house just to make ends meet? As soon as Paul was well she was going to have a long talk with him about it. He did get some foolish, stuffy notions at times.

Carrie wondered if she was being hard in even considering such an event as Paul's demise. Was she perhaps letting her recent discovery of his infidelity color her opinions? Well, why not! she demanded silently. He'd evidently been enjoying quite a Casanova's existence behind her back, hadn't he? Certainly most women would divorce him immediately under the same circumstances . . . wouldn't they? But, she had to concede, most women didn't have a homosexual problem as well. She rested her head in her hands. "Damn it," she muttered. "God damn everything!"

She knew she had forced him into playing around, but it didn't lessen the hurt any. Why did men have to think in terms of sex? Why couldn't companionship and respect ever be enough! But it wasn't, she knew, it just wasn't. And the worst part was that with her past she knew exactly what drove them on; she recalled too often the battle to conceal her hurt when her first lover, Beth, would pull away. Perhaps some bright analyst could explain what happened to people, Carrie thought. She'd not been able to believe that Beth could really love her yet not really want to make love . . . and she supposed Paul felt the same way about her. She was doing precisely the same thing to Paul that Beth had done to her—only Carrie had walked out on Beth because of it. Where had she changed, she wondered; when did I begin to withdraw and why? It was pointless to ask herself these questions. She didn't know and probably would never know the answer. She *did* love Paul; and once in a while she would think that it would be nice to make love—but something stopped her from ever bringing it up, ever making it clear to him that she needed him. She knew it would make him more than just happy if she instigated it, but something held her back. Embarrassment, fear, both? Not that she was truly conscious of—just *something*. Wasn't Paul's solution more mature then? He loved her enough not to force the issue, enough not to impose on her, and enough to never break up their home. He had never let his affairs interfere with his marriage, which was more than she could say for most men. She was well aware that she shouldn't hold it against him, shouldn't feel hurt and betrayed, but she did. She hated herself for the entire situation, and hated him for being the cause of it; she wished they were both seventy years old so that sex would never enter their lives!

If he just weren't so goddamn *good!* she thought. Oh, he was pedantic and often Victorian—but he was basically a kind and gentle man. Even after she'd confessed that she'd married him "on the rebound," he never brought it up again. She sometimes wished he would beat her, or come home drunk. Anything to help her feel less guilty about their marriage. It wasn't fair that she should be the guilty one. All right, so she had been a lesbian; she'd given it up, hadn't she? She didn't play around and make a lie of their marriage the way he did. She didn't . . . "Oh hell, what's the use!" she said.

She suddenly thought of Kim and her immediate reaction was one of not wanting to be bothered with that nonsense right then. It was a healthy reaction, she decided, and just went to show how much she'd changed in the years with Paul. She was a married woman and a mother, not an empty-headed schoolgirl in pursuit of forbidden fruits. Kim was a nice girl, fun to be around, but really, to give her any more importance than that was ridiculous. She'd been so terribly long without any close women friends that she'd forgotten it was possible to just be friends without any sexual undercurrents about it. It had been foolish of her to tell Kim about herself; she'd probably just have to put up with Kim's teasing forever more. But on the other hand, at least she had someone to whom she could talk freely. Carrie finished her second cup of coffee and carried the dishes to the sink to wash. She tried desperately not to bang the heavy iron skillet against the sink since half of their bedroom extended over part of the kitchen. She hoped Paul would wake up before the next morning; she wanted to see his eyes open and feed him something, and know for sure that he was really recovering. Their private problem seemed secondary now.

Paul didn't wake up until six the next morning, but he did seem much more like himself. He was weak and haggard, but he no longer looked like he was at death's door and Carrie didn't know whether she should feel relieved or angry with him for having worried her. She took his breakfast to him, a very light one, and sat down next to the bed. "I don't know why you don't take better care of yourself, Paul. You had me worried sick!"

His dark eyes stared dully back at her. "Just like a woman," he whispered. "Would you mind saving your self-pity until I've gotten over mine? I didn't exactly plan to be sick, y'know."

She let her gaze fall to her lap. "I'm sorry, Paul. Really. I guess I'm still upset." She almost added that it was partly due to having discovered his address book but caught herself in time. It wouldn't do any good to discuss his address book; not then . . . probably never. She had caused it and she had gotten it. Carrie watched him try to eat and finally he gave up. He was already half asleep before she'd even left the room.

Once back in the kitchen she thought she'd better phone Kim before Kim called her and awoke Paul. She dialed the number and felt a little nervous waiting for someone to answer. What if Kim had told George? Or, even if she hadn't but no longer wanted to be her friend? Carrie thought of several what-ifs before Kim finally answered.

"Glad you called," Kim said lightly. "There's a gal at the market that looks an awful lot like a man. Do you suppose she's . . ."

Carrie had to laugh. "I wouldn't know, Kim. Maybe she's just athletic. Anyhow, that's not important right now."

"Some help you are!" Kim said. "I thought you guys were supposed to give off some kind of odor or something by which you could spot each other. . . ."

"Hardly," Carrie answered then changed the subject abruptly. "Listen, Kim, I'm afraid I've got my hands full right now. Paul came home unexpectedly."

"Oh-oh."

"No, nothing like that. He's sick . . . pneumonia."

"Jesus!" Kim said. "Have you called a doctor?"

"Of course. He'll be all right, but I'm afraid my time's going to be rather tied up for awhile." Carrie played with the coiled telephone cord and waited for Kim to make some snide remark. There was a short silence.

"Does he know yet that you know?"

Carrie sighed and was suddenly overwhelmingly tired. "No. What for? I've thought it over rather carefully . . . there's no reason for him to ever know that I've found out. What would it accomplish?"

"Stop being such a damn martyr!" Kim said. "Why the hell should you let him get away with it?"

"Why not? Oh, Kim, don't you see? I've lied to him from the beginning . . . I've not been the right wife for him. I know that sounds corny as all hell, but it's true anyway. How can I now suddenly be self-righteous and . . . oh, never mind. It's too complicated anyway. This whole

90

marriage has been based on lies and deceits. It's too late now."

Kim said nothing for a few seconds. "It's your life, sweetie. Hey, how're you doing on groceries? I've got to go to the market tomorrow anyhow . . . why don't you make out a list and I'll get your stuff at the same time?"

Carrie was completely taken by surprise. It was the last thing she would've expected from Kim and her reaction was a combination of being exceptionally touched, impressed, and skeptical. "That would be a big help, Kim. . . ."

"Well you don't have to sound as if I'd just signed myself into slavery, y'know."

Carrie didn't say anything. She would only embarrass Kim if she thanked her, but inwardly she was delighted. There was hope for Kim yet; it wasn't too late for her to grow up after all.

Paul was in bed for ten days and by the eleventh, she wished to hell he was sick again or at work. What a nuisance men could be, she would remind herself during the day. "Constantly under foot, that's what you are," she'd tell him in mock seriousness and he would laugh. It seemed he did nothing but take food from the refrigerator and flop on the living room couch with his robe on and watch TV. He watched everything from morning quiz programs, noontime serials, and afternoon reruns of last season's comedy shows to the late, late movies; usually asleep by the first third of the latter. No one, she thought, but no one could milk a scene the way men could!

But during Paul's illness, Kim had really knocked herself out. She not only helped with the major marketing so that Carrie wouldn't have to be away from Paul for too long a time, but she even would come over and keep Carrie company during the week. Once she took Sara to Rye Playland and another time to an afternoon movie; both times were the afternoon of Sambo's Scout meeting days when Sara would have no one to keep her company—but more to give Carrie a real rest and some quiet. Sara, of course, adored her and seemed to enjoy just looking at Kim. But Carrie couldn't get over how changed Kim was. She took a deep interest in Sara's upbringing, her interests and games—everything about the child. Both of them would play a game where they pretended to be sisters which left Carrie open to a good deal of teasing from Kim since it made Kim her daughter too.

However, Kim strangely avoided spending any time with Paul as he improved. She was always polite to him, inquired how he felt, but never hung around trying to be social. Carrie could only assume that Kim was probably angry with him for having hurt her, but figured Kim would cool off in time. After all, if Carrie could tolerate the knowledge, she didn't see why Kim couldn't. Carrie herself thought very little about it after that first day or two. She just didn't have the strength to try to solve anything, or rationalize.

At the end of two weeks Paul had popped in and out of the office a couple of times and had made reservations to return to Chicago Sunday night to pick up where he'd left off. Nothing special had happened the first time, he told her. He got off the plane feeling a little woozy and went to the hotel, had a bite to eat and a beer or two in the hotel bar watching the color TV set they had, and went to bed. She hadn't asked with whom. Within a couple of hours he'd known he was seriously sick and with good luck was able to catch a flight right back to New York, wondering all the way if he'd last through the trip. Now he figured he'd had an unexpected two-week vacation and was ready to get back to work—and first things being first, make the trip he should've made.

Carrie tried to feel that she'd miss him but was relieved, with a minimum of guilt, that he'd be gone for the next ten days—she'd earned a little vacation herself. It was just incredible how having one more adult around the house all the time could wear one out so. And, too, it would be fun to resume spending time with Kim again—something she'd not been able to do since Paul's illness—and to get back to work. Work would help take her mind off her marital insecurities. Mr. Arnold had called a few days before asking if she could come into the office one day soon and she'd put him off nicely telling him about her husband and so on. She hadn't the vaguest idea of what Mr. Arnold wanted, but she'd soon find out.

The Sunday of Paul's flight was particularly pleasant. He'd spent a good deal of time with Sambo teaching him how to box, and letting Sara comb his hair—Sara loved to comb her father's hair—and making jokes with Carrie, and telling her how nice she looked. It was a late afternoon flight this time and everything went smoothly and by the time Carrie and the children returned home Carrie indeed believed that God was in His Heaven and all was nearly right with the world. And she was looking forward to the next day, too. She had made an appointment with Mr. Arnold and Kim was coming by for a hamburger dinner with her that evening. It was going to be a nice day.

Chapter VIII

Sambo walked into the kitchen as if by sheer will power he would stand six feet tall. Although he'd resented having to put on a clean shirt and pants earlier, he seemed glad about it now. He brought in the plates from the dining room and put them on the sink next to Carrie—without a word of complaint. Carrie couldn't help a small smile as he reaped the rewards of Sambo's wanting to make a good impression. As the kitchen door swung closed she could barely hear Kim reading to Sara.

"Boy, but she's sure pretty," Sambo said bringing in the last of the dishes. "Boy! I'd of stayed home from Scouts if I'd known."

"Don't you think she looks a little bit like Sara?" Carrie asked suppressing a laugh.

"*Sar*-a! Ah, mom, Sara's just a kid!"

"Kids can be pretty too."

"Not Sara," he said with a finality common between brothers and sisters. "How old do you suppose she is?"

"Six and a half," Carrie joked.

"C'mon, you know who. Mrs. Willis."

"Oh, around twenty-four or so. Never asked her. Why?"

Sambo leaned his elbows on the sink, his chin in his hands. "Just wondered, that's all."

"Well, while you're wondering you've got a choice of drying the dishes for me or going up and taking your shower and getting ready for bed."

"Aw, you're puttin' me on," Sambo cried. Carrie was certain that tonight had been the first time he'd ever heard the expression, or maybe the first time he'd tried to use it at home.

"No, I'm putting you out. Sara's all ready for bed and going up right this minute. The way you fool around you'll be at least another hour yet and it's already eight o'clock. So, what'll it be—dishes or shower?"

"But Mrs. Willis'll think I'm just a kid if I take a shower now."

"No she won't. She'll just know that there's school tomorrow. You don't have to tell her it's grammar school." She watched him turn the possibility of passing for a high school man over in his mind, and his eyes darted to the dishes she washed and was stacking in the drainer. "Besides, you can tell her you've got homework to do . . . that's true enough, isn't it?"

"Yeah," he muttered. "Some dumb book about Switzerland." He thought that over too and after a few moments a slow smile spread over his face. "Y'know, mom . . . you're all right for a girl."

"Thanks, son," she answered seriously. She wiped her hands dry on the dishcloth and followed him through the door into the dining room, past the alcove into the living room where Kim held little Sara next to her, the two of them lying out on the couch. Sara was practically asleep.

"Say, Carrie, this life is pretty great," Kim laughed. "Someone makes you a big dinner, and then you just flake out on the couch while someone does the dishes, and catch up on your reading," she said holding up a battered copy of *Dick Whittington and His Cat* and yawning, "and a clean-smelling little bundle of humanity to keep your bones warm. Yup, I could get used to this."

"Not in this house you wouldn't," Carrie answered. "You're only a guest the first time around. After that, it's help or starve." She turned slyly to Sambo and gave him a meaningful look.

"Oh, yeah. Well, Mrs. Willis," he said stepping forward formally, "I've got school tomorrow," he turned and stole a glance at Carrie, "and some homework before I get to bed yet so I guess I'll have to say good night."

"So soon, Sambo?" Kim said and sat up slowly to disturb Sara as little as possible. "We were just getting to know each other."

"There'll be lots more times, I'm sure," Carrie interceded. "Okay, Sara, it's bedtime for you."

"Come kiss me good night," she whispered and stood up lazily. "Kim's gotta kiss me good night too."

Carrie looked at Kim helplessly, trying to convey the idea that the experience wouldn't be too painful. But Kim didn't seem to mind, in fact, looked genuinely pleased to have been asked. They made an odd little parade up the stairs, led by Sambo of course, and Kim dutifully kissed Sara good night then left the room. Carrie heard her call out another good night to Sambo as she passed his room. Carrie tucked Sara into her bed, switched off the light, gave her a hug and a kiss and then left the room pulling the door halfway closed behind her so the hall light wouldn't keep Sara awake. "No dawdling," she said softly to Sambo as she passed his open bedroom door.

"I won't, Mom," he promised. "Mom?"

"Yes?"

"When will Mrs. Willis come over again?"

She pointed at the pants he'd just left on a chair. "Soon, Sambo."

"Does Dad know her too?" He hung up his pants.

"Yes." She smiled. The Temptress had certainly entered Paul Jr.'s life, all right.

"Wow. She sure is pretty."

"If you like the type," she said in an offhand way.

He grinned. "You are too, but I mean . . ."

"Never mind. I guess I can take your liking another woman."

Sambo—impulsively, she was sure, because he hadn't in ages—ran over to her and threw his arms around her waist. "Good night, Mom."

She scratched the back of his head and answered a soft "Good night," and left his room. By the time she was at the base of the stairs she could hear his shower running. She couldn't stop herself from briefly thinking how nice it was to have the kids and Kim too. How much better, even, than when Paul was home. Women simply understood each other better, that was all. They just did. In a way she regretted that women couldn't marry and have children. But she didn't dare dwell on it and by the time she reached the living room and saw Kim still reading Sara's book she'd forgotten about it.

"All tucked up for the night?" Kim asked and stretched lazily.

"Um-hm," Carrie answered and glanced casually through the paper to see what, if anything, was on TV.

"I don't want to watch TV," Kim said. "Let's put on the radio or records and talk. You've got a phonograph in this museum, haven't you?"

Carrie laughed. "Yes, we managed to save up enough for a victrola back in the 20s."

"Yuk yuk. Any decent records?"

"A stirring collection of the latest 78s," Carrie said loftily and went over to the Do-It-Yourself hi fi set Paul had put together on weekends a few years ago. He'd built the cabinet himself out in the garage and had left ample room for record space, even though they didn't have very many records. The LPs were placed neatly by category under the tuner. Paul liked musicals and light opera and waltzes, Carrie preferred a little more classical music— mostly because she thought the children should be exposed to classical music in the home and because she found it less distracting; otherwise she knew very little about the classics. She'd been meaning for ages to take Sambo, at least, to a live concert, maybe even one of the Saturday afternoon concerts Bernstein conducted for children. Even though she couldn't tell the difference between Liberace and Horowitz, Carrie genuinely enjoyed Chopin and Debussy and Tchaikovsky; Brahms weighed her down a little but she did have a few LPs of varied, popular, selections from the classics and Brahms was always included. Of course, Sambo often spent a whole week's allowance buying the latest pop tunes and at Christmas or his birthday always had records on the list which he laboriously made up at least one month prior, and this he would dispatch with glowing adjectives to his grandmothers and aunts with details of how much he missed them and, incidentally, "in case you were wondering. . . ." The sun rose and fell on The Brothers Four, as far as Sambo was concerned, and Carrie was grateful that he didn't prefer rock 'n roll. It occurred to her that Santa Claus—they still referred to Santa even though Sambo had known for years there wasn't any—might bring Sambo a guitar this Christmas. She'd talk to Paul about it when he came back. It might be nice for Sambo to learn an instrument and, she was sure, Paul would want to assign him certain duties in order to earn music lessons. A guitar was a good boy's instrument, nothing sissy about it like a violin or a flute, and kids who could play an instrument were always more popular in school provided it was a sing-along type of thing. Carrie had no qualms about Sambo's popularity, but she liked to be sure, provide him with little extras in case he didn't make Varsity or something; she was sure that he'd never make a football star because he was so wiry—strong as an ox but on the thin side—but he'd be wonderful in track. He was fast as lightning when he wanted to be, like "not hearing" Carrie if there were chores. She pulled out about five records of mixed music and put them on the machine —Paul had warned her not to stack too many—and smiled to herself as she projected a few years and saw herself sitting in the bleachers cheering Sambo on, waving his school banner, and framing his team photograph (where they were supposed to be relaxed but always trained to have bulging muscles).

"What are you grinning about," Kim said softly over Carrie's shoulder.

Carrie jumped. "Scared the hell out of me," she said. "Why do you go around sneaking up on people?" She laughed a little nervously.

"Didn't sneak up," Kim said and leaned one arm on Carrie's shoulder, her body pressed lightly against Carrie's, "you just didn't hear me." She glanced at the record jackets Carrie'd selected. "No jazz, huh?"

"I hear enough of that at your house," Carrie answered and moved away from Kim, she wasn't quite sure why except for her own guilty feelings and fears. Yet this had been about the fourth or fifth time that Kim had somehow, and certainly innocently enough, come into physical contact with Carrie. A hand on her forearm to emphasize a point, that sort of thing. Perhaps, Carrie thought, I'd just never noticed it before, but she doubted that. "Feel like a drink or something?"

Kim spun around in a graceful pirouette. "Sure. If Paul's stock can take it," she teased, then danced a little bit more.

"I didn't know you were a dancer," Carrie called from the dining room, stopped in front of the liquor cupboard in the ancient buffet, a heavy and ugly mahogany thing complete with traditional mirror on top.

"Didn't you?" Kim executed a rather rusty *glissode assemblé*. "It was mother's idea. She shoved ballet lessons down my throat when I was seven years old, made me study with that lamebrained phony French teacher until I moved to New York." Kim giggled. "Then, out of sheer spite, I started taking lessons with the Martha Graham school," Kim gyrated and flexed her stomach and back muscles wtih incredible control, "had Linda Hodes for my teacher. Ever see Linda dance?"

"No, I've never even heard of Martha Graham." Carrie stood mesmerized watching Kim dance, holding the vermouth and gin bottles by the neck like chickens ready to be plucked.

"Great dancer, really terrific. I'll start following the theatrical section of the *Times* and we'll go see her; you'll love modern dance and especially Linda." Suddenly Kim stopped. "Jesus! am I out of shape!" she laughed. "C'mon, let's go mix those up . . . you couldn't make a good martini if your life depended on it."

Carrie was far more impressed than she knew except that anyone who could dance or was an artist or a musician always awed her, reminded her that all men were not created equal when an honest talent, even a genius, in a particular field were encountered. She followed Kim into the kitchen feeling as if she were the clumsiest thing on two feet—and she felt at that instant that both of hers were probably clubbed. No wonder Kim was always so agile! "Did you ever dance on the stage?" she asked. "Professionally, I mean?"

"Me?" Kim snorted, swearing quietly at the stuck ice-cube tray. "Nah. Never good enough. And, anyway, what for? Your life's never your own, you work your guts out every day keeping in shape and practicing and rehearsing, and they don't pay you enough to cover the cost of lessons. Wasn't the life for me."

"You certainly look like you're good enough."

Kim laughed. "All amateurs think that . . . bet you wouldn't know the difference if the second row was cheating on half-toe. . . ."

Carrie smiled slightly embarrassed. "I wouldn't even know if they were full-toe, whatever that means."

Kim shrugged. "Just shows you." She looked around for glasses and finally found them. "On the rocks or straight?"

"Rocks, thanks."

"Straight life gettin' you down, huh?" Kim roared at her own pun.

"Where the hell did you learn that?" Carrie asked sincerely amused.

"Been reading gay books ever since we had our little talk. I know all about butches, fems, drag queens, rough trade," she smiled impishly. "Most of those novels are pretty ghastly, aren't they?"

Carrie laughed. "You'd know better than I do. The only one I ever read was WELL OF LONELINESS and I was only about twenty or twenty-one then."

"That thing," Kim said, "why that's practically required English Lit . . . for freshman john reading," she added. "I didn't like it."

"Really?" Carrie asked. She'd always thought it a remarkably well-written book.

Kim poured into the pitcher a wrist-flicked amount of vermouth. "Too whiny," she said. "Poor little me, look at me and take pity, I can't help myself. . . ."

"Well, it was written an awfully long time ago. Nobody knew anything much about the subject then."

"I dunno, lots of people suffered from worse mental illnesses then and they didn't go around crying about it."

"Do you think that's all it is? An illness?" Carrie had never really thought of it in those exact terms before, more as an affliction; illness implied you might get well, and it was an interesting approach. Last she'd heard—which was quite a long time, she knew—no one had ever successfully conquered being gay as far as completely getting "well"; they were only successful the way she was, by suppressing it.

"I don't know," Kim laughed easily and carried the pitcher of martinis into the living room and sat down, Carrie took the chair adjoining her, "but from what I've read in those novels most gay people seem to think of it as a God-given way of life; they're *organized* even!" Her hand rested briefly on Carrie's as she said it, then smoothly moved to pour the drinks.

"Well, what's wrong with that?" Carrie asked lifting her glass.

"Nothing, I guess. But who wants to belong to a gay Kiwanis? Next thing you know they'll have a lodge of their own and sell lavender poppies on the street or something."

Carrie had to laugh at the image of daintily dressed fagots mincing up to passers-by on Fifth Avenue with paper flowers in their well-manicured hands; perhaps a little parade would be in order, of course, it would have to be a drag parade. "I think you're being a bit hard on them," she said and liked being able to say "them."

"I don't see why. After all, what would you think if child molesters had their own club, or sadists, or any other sexual perverts?"

"It's not quite the same," Carrie said almost violently. "Homosexuals aren't hurting anyone!"

"Feh! A lot of them are brought out—is that right?—by older people introducing them to it while they're still kids. And even if that's a small proportion it's a proven fact that when homosexuality becomes an accepted and common thing in a society, that society is on the verge of collapse— just look at your history books, at all the ancient civilizations! Decadence is always followed by collapse." Kim sat forward intently trying to make her point with physical gesture as well as words.

"For heaven's sake, Kim, you can't blame all decadence on homosexuality! It's an entire moral collapse, a disregard for current religions, the sanctimony of marriage and family; the ordinary little orgies are equally to blame and there's more of *them!*" She finished off her drink swiftly and poured another. "And economics, too! What national resources did Rome have, or Babylon? Where was industry in Athens? We're changing history within the United States —Mr. Arnold go to hell," she added and they both smiled.

Kim sat back and sighed. "Maybe you're right. But I don't think so. Speaking of the old bastard, what did Arnold want today?"

Carrie snorted. "You wouldn't believe it."

Kim stood up and took off the records, then put on the radio to a jazz station. "Can't stand much more of that crap," she said. "I'll believe it," she added standing next to Carrie and pouring both of them fresh drinks, then sat down on the arm of Carrie's chair.

She was terribly uncomfortable with Kim sitting there, but she couldn't move without pushing Kim's rump off the chair and it would've looked silly. "Well, he gave me a long lecture about how wonderful ARMBREWSTER is, and how American, and offered me a chance to become a part of the permanent staff within the office."

"How much was he offering?"

"That's not the point," Carrie said. "I didn't know if he was stupid or if he thought the kids had gone to live in Oshkosh, but I couldn't take a full-time job at any price."

"Why not? You could get a baby sitter."

Carrie shook her head and silently wished Kim would turn the radio down a little, the jazz was very unnerving right then. "First of all, I wouldn't leave them in the hands of a sitter every day, and secondly, Paul would have a fit."

"Oh Paul-Schmall! When are you going to outgrow him?"

"What do you mean," Carrie said slowly.

"When's the last time you had any real fun, Carrie? Have you ever had an affair since you got married? Or gone on a vacation alone where you could do as you pleased? He hasn't exactly deprived himself of kicks all this time. . . ."

"But I don't want to," she answered seriously, if not a little impatiently. The radio was now playing the same kind of music that Kim and that Kingsley ape had been dancing to and Carrie didn't think she could take much more. "Couldn't we turn that down a little," she said started to stand up, Kim's rump or no.

"Sure," Kim answered and walked over to the radio. "Mix up another batch, will you? Like I showed you?"

Carrie was already on her way into the kitchen and called a "Yes" back. She pulled out fresh cubes and wondered about Kim's question. Did she really not want to have affairs, or was it just part of her over-all suppression of anything which might conflict with her life as a wife and mother? She wasn't really too certain now. It hadn't come up before, she supposed, because she'd never been in a position to choose; what man had approached her besides George, and she couldn't count him. Was she missing something? Certainly if the polls were anything to go by, she was one of the last of the Puritans about fidelity; simply everyone had affairs, everyone—unless they were religious fanatics or something. Even Paul, though she admitted for perhaps different reasons. What was she trying to prove? But then, she asked herself, who would I not prove it with anyhow? She smiled at her own lack of moral rebellion and returned to the living room. Kim was doing the "fish" all alone.

"Know how?" Kim asked as she poured the drinks.

"No," Carrie smiled. "At lease, not standing up."

Kim laughed. "C'mon, I'll show you."

Carrie had a moment of hesitation about dancing with Kim, especially something as intimate as "fish", but she watched Kim dancing and suddenly felt very reckless and carefree. When Kim opened her arms out in invitation, Carrie walked into them. There was nothing to learn, really; if she could lift her heels off the floor, stay in one spot, gyrate her pelvis in time, then she was "fishing."

"Hey, you learn pretty fast," Kim said. "The kids all think this dance is dead, but that's because they dance it straight. I'll show you dirty fish now." Kim shot one leg in between Carrie's legs and without losing time to the music used her upper thigh to rub against Carrie's vagina while her breasts moved across Carrie's in a slow, teasing sideways motion. Her arms locked behind Carrie's back and she put her face next to Carrie's so that her heavy breathing was on Carrie's ear. Carrie could smell the perfume on Kim's neck, and her nose was almost in Kim's hair with its soft fresh aroma.

"You do it to me too," Kim breathed.

Carrie didn't have to be told, all she did was move an inch closer and her leg was between Kim's. She broke out in a light perspiration and if the music didn't stop soon she thought she might come; it was the most agonizing feeling she'd ever had and she didn't want it to stop or to go on—either one was torture. At first she didn't really believe it but as Kim's lips moved against her neck and down to her shoulders, her teeth taking teasing bites from her flesh, Carrie suddenly lost eleven years, lost all idea of where she was or with whom except that it was doubly

103

exciting after so long, and knowing that it was Kim, not the Kim of the sarcastic remarks but a new Kim of her own, a passionate, taunting, demanding, hot, rounded and womanly Kim.

"Don't stop dancing," Kim whispered and brought her face up to Carrie's. She looked at Carrie for a long time, her lips pulling a little as they parted and came nearer and nearer, then finally touched Carrie's lips, softly, gently, probingly, and after hour-long seconds Kim traced Carrie's lips with her tongue, going into her mouth a little more with each circle, darting and light, resting briefly under Carrie's tongue and suddenly pushing deep into her mouth uniting like two hot and wet snakes rolling around each other. And all the while Kim's legs pushed against Carrie, so close that Carrie could feel through Kim's pants to the soft mound of pubic hair and felt the moisture coming through on her own thighs.

"Good God, Kim," Carrie said hoarsely, "I can't take much more of this."

"Upstairs?" she whispered.

"No. Here, where I can look at you. I want to see your breasts, your belly, I want to. . . ."

"Waste not, want not," Kim said slyly and still dancing began to unbotton her blouse.

Carrie helped her undress and took a delightful, avaricious pleasure in knowing what was coming, in watching Kim boldly undress before her and then helping Carrie undress. She enjoyed a frenzy of sexual lust she'd never felt before and didn't even know how they reached the large old sofa, what the radio was playing, or anything other than the sweet, sweat-salty taste of Kim's breasts.

"You're wet," Kim said barely audibly.

"You're damn right," Carrie answered. "You are too."

"Make me wait, I want to wait as long as I can. . . ."

Chapter IX

There was no excuse for it, Carrie told herself over and over the next morning—just no excuse at all! It was not only stupid and foolish, but so damn dangerous in the living room like that. What if Sambo had come downstairs, or Sara, or if Paul had come home unexpectedly again. What? She berated herself for all kinds of a fool and no sooner would she be in complete accord with her self-accusations than she'd start a fresh onslaught of recriminations. She hadn't even been drunk! Oh, Kim had been clever about it, there was no denying that and it had been clearly Kim's plan rather than her own. She was glad that Kim had gone home last night, relieved that she wouldn't have to face her now. She wouldn't know what to say or how to behave. Maybe Kim had been drunk even if she hadn't. "I should of stopped it, I should of refused to dance, I should've . . ." Carrie's voice trailed off into a hopeless silence and she lay in the big double bed very still as if the sheets themselves would accuse her if she moved. Suddenly she recalled the scene in the kitchen that day she'd told Kim about her past; what was it Kim had said then? Not her cup of tea? No, that she wasn't *cut out for that sort of thing,* that was it. But Carrie also remembered how Kim had said she loved her. What had she meant? Carrie strained to recreate the entire scene in her mind. She said "love," not *"in* love," she couldn't have meant anything else . . . could she?

"Shit!" Carrie muttered, "shit, shit, shit!" She sat up in bed and squinted at the small alarm clock on the night stand. Six-thirty. The kids would be waking up soon and there was breakfast to make, and lunches to fix before they left; they'd just have to take their lunches today; she couldn't bring herself to have them running in and out at noon. Not today. If there were only some place she could

105

leave them for a day or two, just long enough to get her thoughts in order. But their aunts and grandmothers were too far away and for once Carrie regretted it. Paul's family lived in dead New Bedford and only New England stubbornness kept the town from rigor mortis; they were nice people, his family, but a terse, dry family group with a Victorian morality. And her own family, what was left of it, was in Atlantic City; not a much warmer bunch than Paul's. Maybe it was tough on Kim that her parents had each remarried, but at least her parents were alive, were willing to face facts and seek a change. But then, what difference did it make when the chips were down? Kim, with her background, and Carrie with hers, and both of them on the couch making love. She'd never made love to anyone like Kim before and it had been more than just exciting. Kim talked constantly; gave directions, or a running report on what it felt like and what she wanted to do to Carrie until, despite the narrow couch, they found a comfortable mutual working arrangement. Carrie had known women, some few, who groaned and writhed as she herself did, but never anyone like Kim. It was a lesson Carrie didn't think she'd ever forget and even now, her guilts and derisions aside, she was getting hot again. She'd not had to worry whether she was going too fast or too slow, too heavy or too light—Kim kept her perfectly informed so that there was none of the awkwardness trying to discreetly find out what your partner liked best, or where, or how. Blueprint for love, Carrie thought lewdly and thoroughly enjoyed it. Oh, women do understand each other better, she reaffirmed, they definitely do. The soles of Carrie's feet were getting hot and tingly, along with the rest of her, so she quickly lit a cigarette and got up. This was no way to chastize herself! Briefly, a sense of shame pervaded her but it was more because she was capable of such passion but not with Paul.

She threw on an old pair of slacks and enjoyed the worn-soft feel of the material against her skin. She felt bodily clean, washed and well-known; a feeling she'd forgotten since her marriage to Paul, since intercourse with a man. It was so different with a woman, she never felt she was "getting screwed" with either of its meanings; instead she always felt she'd "made love." No doubt it was foolish, Carrie conceded silently, and it was probably that reaction that separated the queers from the straights, but there it was. She slipped quietly through the hall and down the stairs into the kitchen and noiselessly put on the kettle for coffee. Carrie didn't know why she was being so quiet, the kids only had about five or ten more minutes to sleep before they had to start getting ready anyhow. The kids, she thought. The kids and Paul. Was she now an adulteress? Infidelity didn't have to be with someone of the opposite sex, did it? "Oh, good God I was stupid!" she said to the stove. What would Kim think of her now? But then, she had to admit after a moment, she wasn't really so very concerned about what Kim's moral attitude would be. No. What she was really worried about was whether or not Kim had enjoyed making love with a woman; did it measure up to her other experiences with men, that was her concern. Not a very safe reaction after eleven years on the straight and narrow.

Sounds of first one alarm, then another, and shuffles, then running water, left Carrie no time for further thought on the incident. There was breakfast to be made. Even though Sara didn't have to be in school until half an hour after Sambo, they always left together so he could help her across the streets and she'd remain on the playground with the other children until school began. It was an unnerving breakfast with Sambo chattering on about Kim, asking questions. Carrie, at one point, had an urge to tell him to never mind, that his mother had cornered the market, but naturally had to control it. Finally they were off and the house was quiet. So wonderfully quiet. Carrie sat down heavily at the table with a second cup of coffee and just let the hot liquid seep through her body hoping for some drop of energy to come forth from it.

As she might have expected, the phone rang rudely. She went over to it and lifted the receiver, "Hello?"

"Hi."

It was Kim and the sound of her voice that early in the morning surprised Carrie so much she forgot to be uncomfortable.

"I'm so sore I can hardly sit down," she laughed. "How many'd you use anyway? . . .

Carrie could feel her face turning red and was too embarrassed to say anything.

"Doing anything important right now?"

"No," Carrie answered. "Just finished getting the kids off."

"I'll be right over, unless," she paused, "you intend to yell at me again."

"No. No. I won't yell at you, Kim. I'm too tired."

"Me too," Kim said cheerfully. "See you in a jiffy."

Carrie smiled as she hung up the receiver. Kim's using the word "jiffy" would be like Sambo saying "Odds bodkins." So here we go again, thought Carrie as she went through the same routine gestures she had that other Saturday, even to the same kind of thoughts almost. Only this time there was very little doubt in her mind that she would continue to see Kim; she had to. Carrie didn't dare guess what the eventual outcome of all this would be; she didn't even want to. But for all her repulsion at committing adultery, she had to have Kim. She was in love with her, period. They'd have to be discreet from now on, of course; no more idiotic couch scenes. But they'd manage. That is, if Kim felt the same way about her. . . . Yet it was impossible! Utterly impossible. Discreet indeed. You could never be discreet about an affair; you could just hope you didn't get caught. And if they were discovered? Kim had very little to lose, but Carrie would lose the children, ugly scenes in court, shame piled upon shame. She could, in defense, bring countercharges against Paul; but the whole idea appalled her. Carrie gave up. She just didn't know what she would do or even what she *could* do!

She heard Kim's car drive up and for a split second had that same feeling she'd had when she first met Kim: the panic and the urge to run, to hide. But she wouldn't and she knew it. She was surprised to see Kim in a dress instead of slacks. "Not only up at this hour," Carrie said as she came in, "but dressed too. How come?"

"Told George I had an appointment with the hairdresser first thing and that I was going to spend the day with some old cronies from Warrensburg who were in town for the next few days."

"Any special reason?"

"Sure. I don't want him getting on my tail for the next few days and little by little I want to break him into the idea of my spending more time away from home, eventually even evenings."

"I'm afraid I don't quite. . . ."

"George is always checking up on me," she sighed. "He doesn't care much what I do as long as he knows all about it, and he's always afraid I'm holding back something."

"Like last night," Carrie asked hesitantly.

"Yeah," Kim said and kissed her lightly on the lips, "and many more to come. Gad! what a pun!"

Then she did feel the same way! Carrie thought. While there'd been a chance that it was a fluke occasion Carrie hoped she'd be spared the decision of what to do about her feelings toward Kim. But now? "Look, Kim," she began slowly, "just what is on your mind?"

"What do you mean?" Kim found another cup, brought the coffee pot to the table, and sat down. "Should be plain. I had a great time last night, the best in ages, and I want to be sure I can get more." She brought the cup to her lips and blew on the hot coffee.

"Is that all last night meant to you, Kim? Kicks? Something new that you'll dump when it wears off?" Carrie waited for Kim's answer, torn between wanting her to answer yes and also no.

Kim shrugged. "I don't believe in examining sex closely. You start analyzing things and you take all the romance out of it, y'know what I mean? While it's good, it's good. . . ."

"And what about love, Kim?"

Kim stared at her for a few seconds with an unreadable expression. "Love?"

"Love."

109

"But I've already told you I loved you, told you again last night." She said it in a pouting, put-upon way.

"No you didn't," Carrie said evenly. "You only said that you loved *it,* you didn't say what *it* was."

Kim stood up and came over to her side and kissed her again. "Silly nut, of course I love *you* and meant *you.* You're such a naive romantic, Carrie. Want me to retrieve your hanky from the lion's den too? Spread my Oleg Cassini over the mud puddles for you to walk on? Don't know why I should be the butch when you've got all the experience," she added laughing.

Carrie smiled and was reassured. "I've never believed in that kind of distinction. If one of us has to be a man why bother to be gay?" Kim had pulled her to her feet and stood against her with her arms around Carrie's neck, using Carrie's body as a platter for her own. Carrie didn't know what perfume Kim was wearing, but it gave her a heady feeling, a desire to push herself right through Kim.

"How about a morning round-up," Kim suggested softly.

"It's insane to do that here in the house, Kim," she said but didn't sound very firm even to herself. "The kids walking in and out . . . Paul might come home. . . ."

"Kids are in school and Paul's out of town."

"But you never know, kids get sniffles and are sent home. . . ."

"We'll go upstairs and lock the door," Kim said with a broad smile on her face, "pretend you went back to bed if the phone rings or anything, which is true enough."

"But. . . ."

"More, baby, more. I didn't get up at this hour to talk!"

*　　*　　*　　*

Kim rolled over on her back and stretched languidly. "Um, that was just what the doctor ordered . . . of course, he was a queer doctor. . . ."

"Cigarette?" Carrie said taking one for herself.

"Not right now, thanks. What time is it anyway?" She

110

rolled over on her right side facing Carrie carelessly letting the sheet tangle around her small waist.

Carrie looked at the clock. "Little past ten-thirty. Sleepy?" She cupped her hand underneath one of Kim's breasts and fondled it gently. With all her make-up gone she really did remind her of Sara; she hoped she was not acting out some sort of incestuous transference, or whatever they called it.

"Kids coming home for lunch?"

"Hm? Oh, no, they took their lunch today."

"That's good." She lazily rested her leg across Carrie's pelvis. "You've the most beautiful breasts I've ever seen."

Carrie laughed. "Not any more, I'm afraid. Two kids, y'know."

"Did you breast-feed them?'

"Uh-huh."

"Selfish little monsters! I'm jealous."

Carrie leaned over closer and offered her breast to Kim, stroked her hair as Kim kneaded her breast and sucked on it.

"I don't mind your not having any milk," Kim said after a moment with Carrie's nipple still in her mouth," but couldn't you manage one little martini in there?"

"Fresh out," Carrie said. "An early lunch do?"

"I'd rather a late breakfast . . . I'm starved!"

"Eggs over easy and link sausage?"

Carrie slid out of bed and got dressed again. She turned before leaving the room to go downstairs and was momentarily startled to see Kim there instead of Paul. It was a strange feeling. Little Kim lost in the large bed instead of Paul sprawled out like a Michelangelo anatomy lesson; it seemed proper and fitting that Kim should be there; it wasn't a chore to make her breakfast or do anything else for her. No doubt it was because the whole concept of taking care of a woman after eleven years with a man brought back her earlier affairs, she thought, as she left the room. It was always easier to live with a woman; they didn't demand as much or resent having to do dishes; she could say she had the premenstrual blues and know that she was understood, that a woman didn't think she was making it up or giving in to a whim; she could say she didn't feel like cooking and know that the other girl wouldn't mind cooking. So many small, seemingly insignificant things about daily life that became more pleasant with a woman who shared it with her instead of a man who considered it his due. Of course, she knew, a woman didn't support her which, after all, made a difference. There had been Adele, tall and willowy and very quiet; she had been a one-girl office for a manufacturer's representative. Mandy, an intense, wiry girl who wanted to be an actress and devoted all her time outside her job in a steno pool to it. And, of course, Beth, her first lover. The most turbulent, exciting, death-hold affair of all. Beth had been quite a woman, all right. Almost sixteen years ago, Carrie realized with a shock. Where was Beth now . . . married? Still in gay life? All of them . . . where were they now? It was strange about gay affairs and why they broke up—she herself never completely remembered what caused each breakup; they just happened. With hindsight she could recall some over-all damning reason, but that was never accurate. It would be easy to say, well, one was bitchy, the other frigid—as she'd learned the hard way so many lesbians are—and so on, but these things were seldom the real reason, and she was not schooled enough in psychology to analyze what the truth might be. For that matter, she reasoned silently, I don't suppose even the psychiatrists really know.

"Hey, smells good in here," Kim said standing in the doorway watching her. She was dressed again, but hadn't bothered to put on fresh make-up. Kim walked over to the stove and leaned over the frying sausages. "I could eat a ton of 'em!"

"Thought I might baste the eggs instead; like them that way?"

"You're cooking," Kim said and gave her a light hug around the waist. "Surprise me."

Carrie laughed and disengaged herself from Kim's arms. "Go 'way, brat, I'm busy."

Kim sat down at the table and played with the handle of the sugar bowl. "God I hate to think of going home."

"Shall I ask why before I decide to be flattered?"

"No," Kim said. "Go ahead and be flattered. I like it being here with you alone. . . ."

Carrie smiled to herself. It was the first kind of nonsexual remark Kim had made, the first inkling that Kim cared for her as a person as well. And it was high time, too. She dreaded the thought of the children coming home and spoiling it all, and what would they do when Paul was back? She must remember to change the sheets right away, before Paul came home, in fact she would do it right after breakfast to play it safe. It had to be the last time they made love in the house, the absolute last time. And it wasn't just that she might get caught, but more that having an affair in Paul's home, in the children's home, really disturbed her morally. If she had to have an affair at all, the least she could do would be to respect the sanctimony of her other life; if she must betray there was no reason to flaunt it. Even Paul had shown that much courtesy.

"Does George ever stay over night in Manhattan?" she asked Kim suddenly while serving their breakfast.

"Sure," Kim said. "Two, three times a month because he's worked late and the other times," she laughed, "when he's got some broad to screw. A few of his packed suitcases for business trips never leave the office, I'm sure."

"That helps."

"Helps what?" Kim said and picked up a sausage with her fingers.

Carrie sat down opposite her. "Well, we can't go on making love here in the house, that's all. It's too dangerous and I really can't relax."

"You do all right for someone who can't relax!"

"Be serious, Kim. Bad enough we're adulteresses, worse that we're lesbian adulteresses, but I don't like the idea of using my children's home for that purpose, or Paul's bed."

"Adulteresses!" Kim said and burst out laughing. "You can't be cheating on your husband if you're sleeping with a woman!"

"That's a debatable point, Kim, but in any event this house is off-limits from now on. If it were just our husbands I don't think I'd care so much, but not with the kids around. They didn't ask to have me as their mother and I won't risk them walking in on us one day."

"Who's going to walk in? Jesus, Carrie, this is no time to start getting on your mother kick again. Face facts. You're a les, you're married and you've got kids. Enjoy yourself. Have everything. You always louse things up when you begin to worry. It's your house as much as theirs, you work as hard as Paul does to keep family fed and happy . . . if Paul can screw around, why can't you?"

"At least, not in this house," Carrie answered getting mildly annoyed with Kim's lack of comprehension or sensitivity. "And, quite frankly, I've told you that it isn't Paul's fault . . . not really."

"You don't know much about men, sweetie. They *all* do it. I could tell you stories that would make your hair curl. Y'know, Carrie, for being a lesbian you're awfully naive. Paul just has a better excuse than most men. Even if you two screwed every day, he'd *still* fool around!"

Carrie pondered a moment. "I doubt that."

Kim leaned forward and took a more patient tone. "What do you want us to do, go to motels all the time? I don't know about you, but my household allowance won't stretch that far and we can't charge it at Macy's!"

"I've my job," Carrie said triumphantly, "it's enough to carry us through if we want to meet when George is at home."

"Then what do you tell precious Paul when he asks what you've done with all the money you earned."

Carrie had no answer for that and she looked completely crestfallen, apparently enough to stir Kim. "All right, Carrie. From now on it'll be at my house or a motel, but I'm not taking the whole burden. I don't want George to catch us either."

"I wouldn't want you to, Kim. We'll work out something." She felt greatly relieved that Kim had capitulated, and very grateful. She wondered if Kim would've given in a month before. She'd changed so much since Paul's illness. All she'd needed was to be needed; Carrie was certain of that.

"Well, I suppose it doesn't matter much whose husbands finds out . . . either way it's curtains for both of us. Anyhow, we may peter out and not have to worry about it," Kim said lightly.

"Don't say that, please," Carrie asked. "I need you Kim, I'm in love with you." She felt it so strongly as she said it that she was on the verge of tears.

"You're a real kook, y'know that? I was only kidding."

"Well, not even in kidding. If what we have now has to end I'll face it when it happens. I don't want to think about it now."

"Hey, what time is it?" Kim asked and glanced at the kitchen clock. "Jesus! I've got to get out of here."

"I thought you were spending the day," Carrie asked surprised.

"Hell no! I've got to find a hairdresser if my story's to stick with Georgie-Porgie." She jumped up from the table and found her purse, kissed Carrie lightly on the cheek and thanked her for the breakfast, and ran out the door. It was all so sudden, so completely unexpected, that Carrie barely realized she'd gone afterwards. It took her several minutes to adjust to Kim's whirlwind exit, and even longer to justify it in the only way she could . . . that Kim was, indeed, just a child.

Chapter X

Until the day of Paul's return, the two women saw each other constantly and spent probably more time in bed than out of it. In fact, they had begun to joke about whether or not they'd recognize each other dressed. However Carrie's edict that they should not make love in her house had not been adhered to very well. For one reason or another, Kim always had some valid reason why they couldn't go to her house, or more subtly she would arouse Carrie beyond the point of waiting another minute, certainly not long enough to get in a car and find a motel. Besides, though Carrie was afraid to admit it to Kim, the whole idea of presenting themselves at a motel, with a New York license plate, and taking a room for a few hours only . . . well, it was a very awkward picture and one which Carrie dreaded with embarrassment. Kim didn't have to work very hard to arouse Carrie sexually; where Kim was concerned Carrie's glands were in nearly superhuman health, which led to a great deal of intimate ribbing from Kim. In fact, Kim was working on an experiment she'd read in some novel; each time Carrie reached orgasm Kim would say a particular word—she'd chosen the word "hole"—and was working on the theory that eventually she'd have Carrie so conditioned that she'd be able to just say the word at any time and Carrie would have an orgasm. It mildly irked Carrie on occasion that Kim could be so clinical at a time like that, but not enough for her to object verbally; and, too, she had to admit that even in such a short time if she heard the word her pulse was responding a little. She doubted that the experiment would ever be successfully proven; she was entirely too self-conscious a person for something of that sort.

All in all, there seemed to be very little else to deepen their relationship. Whenever Carrie would try to draw out Kim's past, her deeper thoughts, Kim would always change the subject or make some comment that there wasn't anything to tell, or just laugh and shrug. Most of the time Kim kept Carrie in conversation revolving solely around homosexuality—it seemed to absorb her, fascinate and excite her. She'd been pleading with Carrie to take her to a lesbian nightclub so she could see the lesbians first hand. This attitude of Kim's annoyed Carrie, her obsession to "see the lesbians" reminded Carrie of some kind of side-show neurotic, but when she'd comment on Kim's attitude she'd quickly explain that she didn't mean it the way it sounded.

"I don't want to feed the freaks bananas," Kim would assure her, "it's just that I'm curious to know more about

116

lesbians." Carrie tried to explain to her that in all likelihood the clubs she had frequented eleven years ago were closed up by now. Except for the 82 Club downtown, which was just a tourist spot, all the real gay club were constantly being closed down and new clubs would spring up. She'd have a heck of a time finding a new club she knew; after all, she couldn't call up some bar and ask if they still catered to the gay crowd! There had been the *Wishbone,* long closed and now something else; the *Grapevine,* now run by some kind of a political organization. Without contacting some of her former gay friends, she'd never find a club. But Kim was adamant . . . did Carrie really think she could locate these former friends? That would be even better, Kim would argue, they might even double-date. . . .

Naturally, Carrie never mentioned it to Kim, but she was almost looking forward to Paul's return, to some semblance of a routine again. Kim was a demanding personality, and at times, even a tiring one—much as she loved Kim. As it was she had already refused one assignment from Mr. Arnold in order to be with Kim as much as possible, to take advantage of Paul's absence, but Carrie didn't want to give a bad impression to Mr. Arnold, didn't want him to think that she was getting too big for her britches and start being temperamental about when she'd work and when she wouldn't. Bad enough she'd been forced to refuse accepting his offer of a permanent staff job. But on the other hand, with Paul's return, she didn't know how she was going to look him in the eye, how she'd be able to endure his caresses, much less how she'd live without Kim every single day. Paul would be bound to notice a change in her, something different. On the following Sunday she received a wire from Paul saying he was in Minnesota, was going to circle down through the south, his last stop being Columbus, Georgia, and then would return home on Friday, just a few days more than his anticipated 10-day trip. He never wrote or telephoned when he was away but did always wire in advance when he'd be home again. Carrie wondered how many names were in Paul's book for Minnesota and Columbus, but she no longer really cared. She had Kim.

The Thursday afternoon before his arrival Kim had finally wheedled Carrie into calling an old friend of hers in Manhattan. Louise had been more than a little surprised to hear from Carrie after all those years, but had sounded pleased if not a little concerned about Carrie's return to a gay relationship. But Carrie assured her all was well, and that she wanted Louise to meet Kim and why didn't they all get together one evening and go out to a gay club in celebration of their reunion. They fixed a date for the Saturday a week after Paul's return—she'd tell him that she was going to the theater with Kim, or something. And even though Kim pouted that she needn't have made the date so far away, she was pacified that at least they were going to go and didn't pester Carrie anymore about it; except to remind her that if she'd not been so stubborn about it they could have gone while Paul was still away. It was impossible to make Kim understand that she hadn't wanted to contact Louise simply to find out the name of a gay club, that it was unfair to the close friendship they had once had. The whole thing made her feel disloyal and sneaky, but she'd done it and that was that.

Friday afternoon, Carrie and the children piled into the Nash and drove out to LaGuardia to meet Paul's flight. It was an overcast day and had rained a little two or three times already. She hoped his flight wouldn't be delayed because of the weather; Carrie didn't share the children's enthusiasm for the airport, much less the unnerving drive and hassle to find a place to park, always followed by what seemed a three-mile hike to the terminal. She would have preferred that Paul spend the $5.00 for a cab to the house, or even take the less expensive limousine to White Plains and pick him up there; but it was one of the few things he asked of her and he did seem to relish the thought of coming back and being met by his family—one of the rare romantic fancies he had and she didn't have the heart to deny him. By four-thirty they were walking into the terminal and had a half-hour to kill before his flight was due to arrive. She checked with the ticket counter and they assured her his plane was on time, then took the children to the rather depressing restaurant on the second floor. All three had sodas and watched the planes land and take off. Carrie tried desperately to be animated, to give Sambo and Sara the impression that she was as eager to see their father as they were, but thoughts of Kim and their intimacy made it difficult, and the fear and guilt of facing Paul made it almost impossible. He didn't deserve to have a scandal like that in his life and, even though Kim would insist that it couldn't be a scandal until everyone knew about it, it was an awful burden for Carrie. She could still remember her mother telling her that she should never do anything she wouldn't want the whole world to know. . . .

But the nasal female voice on the loudspeaker announced the arrival of Paul's flight and they hastily went to the specified gate which didn't leave Carrie much time to think about anything else. Apparently the plane had not carried a full passenger load and Paul was among the first people off. He smiled and waved when he spotted them and increased his pace until he reached them. He embraced Carrie and kissed her briefly—for which she was oddly miffed—and then concentrated his attention on the children before they went to collect his luggage. What if he did have affairs, Carrie wondered, she was not in any position to wrangle now—she was even more guilty. Walking to the car, Sambo carrying Paul's briefcase and Sara helping her father carry the suitcase, Paul seemed more than ordinarily talkative. "I tell you, hon, I hit some of those accounts just in the nick of time. You know how they get when you can't court 'em every day, or be right on tap for all their little questions . . . why ol' man Matthew seemed actually hurt that I hadn't come by sooner to see the new plant . . . as if I had nothing else to do but go around the country breaking champagne bottles over new factories," he laughed. "But it's good to be home, it really is. I really don't know how most people can live in those small towns, I really don't. Nothing to do, movie houses showing only Westerns, bars closed at nightfall just about. Give me New York anytime!"

"Did you bring presents?" Sara demanded.

119

"Sara!" Carrie said. "That not nice to say when you haven't seen your father in so long. . . ."

Paul smiled at Carrie over the top of Sambo's head with an expression of the tolerant father. "It's a natural enough question . . . and," he turned his face toward Sara, "yes, I did bring you a little present. Just a little one, though; not much room for things in suitcases and especially with excess baggage charges."

"Well, it sounds as if you had a profitable trip all right."

"Pretty much so. Got that contract from the concrete company, and lit a fire under that plastics factory to put some ads in *Market Management* magazine. People are really funny, y'know? Big rich companies spend lots of money to hire an ad agency but won't spend a dime for ads. . . ."

They reached the car and climbed in, paid the attendant, and in amazing time for that hour of the day were on the turn-off from Grand Central Parkway onto Northern Boulevard. "Anybody for a quick stop at Jahn's for an ice cream?" Paul asked.

The children agreed readily but Carrie said, "They both just had sodas, Paul, and with the traffic right now. . . ."

"Okay, kids, next time," Paul decreed to a duet of "Aw." "Kids been giving you a rough time, Carrie? You look tired and seem kind of jumpy."

"No," she answered softly. "Not really. Not any more than usual, anyway," she added with a forced smile. "I'm just tired. Might be catching a cold or something."

He nodded. "Well, when we get home you take a long hot bath and I'll fix us a drink before dinner. Maybe Sambo and I could rustle up some eggs or something so you won't have to cook. How's that." He placed his right hand on her forearm and patted it gently.

She didn't want him to do anything for her and his being so nice was unreasonably infuriating her. But Carrie didn't dare refuse his kindness, mostly because it would hurt his feelings, but also did not want to arouse any suspicions about her state of mind. She wished he'd come home in a bad mood so that she wouldn't have to see his cheerful expression, his delight at being with his family again. She couldn't help feeling like a coward, a two-timing whore with no right to a husband like Paul much less the children. Oh, she knew it was considered square to have a conscience, but there it was anyway and it plagued her, tormented her. If she could just hate Paul, even a little bit, if he just wasn't so nice it would all be so much simpler. But he loved her and trusted her and she had betrayed him, and what was worse, knew that she would continue to betray him, that she didn't have the guts to break off with Kim. His own transgressions didn't count anymore.

The traffic on the Whitestone Bridge was heavy but at least it moved and within an hour they were walking into the kitchen of their home. For a second Carrie almost expected to see Kim sitting at the table, for no valid reason other than having been with her so much lately. The house seemed different to her as they entered and Paul, followed by the children, took his suitcase upstairs while she sat down in the living room. She sat in the same chair she'd sat in the night she and Kim had "fished;" had done more than that. Was it really only ten days before? So much, so much had happened; the furniture seemed strange, everything looked like a memory from a dream rather than her own home she knew so well. She could hear Paul talking to the kids upstairs, and their laughter, and wondered what she was doing in that house—that she didn't belong there any more than a frog in a desert. She wondered too how long this feeling of being an alien would last, if she'd ever get used to the double life, calloused to it so that she could continue the deceit without guilt. She didn't know, wouldn't know perhaps until Lord knew how long.

Paul had changed his clothes and was wearing his faded denim pants and a sports shirt as he came down the stairs. "Sambo's grown, y'know that?" He laughed and came and sat down on the couch—Kim's couch, Carrie thought heavily.

"It's hard to tell when you see them everyday," she answered.

Paul stretched. "It's great being back," he said. "Guess

121

I'll never understand how some men can enjoy being away from home, unless," he laughed, "they're not happy at home. The only good thing about these trips—other than money, of course—is that they always remind me of how lucky I am. See those men sitting in bars getting drunk, staring at television sets when they could be home with their families . . . what a waste of time, huh?"

"You never were one for being a tourist," she said vaguely, not able to prevent thinking, at least, that he was omitting his little amusements while gone.

"That's not what I mean and you know it," he teased, then said more seriously. "You do look rather pale, Carrie. Got a temperature?" He stood up and placed his hand on her forehead.

"No, Paul. I told you, I'm just tired."

He kissed her on the cheek and helped her to her feet. "You go take a bath . . . g'on now, do as I tell you. I'll mix us a cocktail and then you come downstairs in a warm robe and bundle up here on the couch. Anything special in the house you'd like for dinner?" He put his arms around her waist and held her lightly.

She had a horrible feeling of claustrophobia in his arms but didn't dare yield to it. "I'm not too hungry. . . ."

"Little cocktail'll fix that . . . still like martinis?"

"Yes, Paul, thanks." She agreed with him, would have agreed to anything at that moment just to have him release her, leave her alone. "There's a big sirloin I bought today; they were on sale."

"Great! What do you do to it, just mash some garlic on it?"

Carrie nodded and thought she'd faint if he didn't let her go soon. "You should do it now, Paul. Let it sit at room temperature with the garlic for about an hour or so."

He gave her an affectionate pat on the behind and said, "Your wish is my command. Go take that bath, okay?"

Carrie tried to keep a sigh of relief out of her voice as she began walking toward the stairs. "I won't be too long," she said, then paused as she took the first step. "Paul . . ."

she called tentatively. She'd been unforgivably rude since he'd deplaned.

"Yes hon?"

"I'm . . . I'm glad you're home." It surprised her that, in a way, she meant it.

He grinned boyishly. "Go take your bath."

*   *   *   *

By the following Saturday Carrie was in a state of nerves she didn't dare admit. She lived in constant suspense and horror that Paul might realize it was more than a pending cold that was making her so irritable. She tried desperately not to let it show, to keep control of herself, but it was almost impossible. She'd been given another assignment by ARMBREWSTER, and Sara had a slight case of the flu and was in bed for two days, and Paul seemed to be going out of his way to spend more time at home in the evenings —that would wear off soon, she knew, but in the meantime having him around was driving her nearly insane. She'd hardly seen Kim and though this was the Saturday they were going into town to meet Louise—Paul had readily agreed to staying with the children alone and giving her an evening out—she wished that Kim would call and say that they should cancel out, that they should find a motel instead and just be near each other, touch each other; something to indicate that Kim had really missed her and needed her, if only half as much as Carrie needed her. But instead Kim had called excitedly to confirm their evening out and Carrie couldn't help feeling somewhat hurt. Kim was so very young, though, Carrie rationalized. She couldn't honestly expect Kim to completely understand what it was like to be in love, to be dependent on someone, to always, always want to be near; she'd learn in time, of course, but being able to love someone completely is a cultivated virtue.

Kim picked her up at a quarter of seven and rather than come in the house simply honked for her to come out. Carrie wore a simple black dress that wasn't too dressy; after all, she had to make it look as if she were really going to the theater but didn't want to be overly dressed and cause suspicious comment in a gay club. She felt very proud of herself and knew she looked unusually attractive as she kissed the kids good night.

"You look very pretty tonight," Paul said standing at the front door, "almost wish I were going with you."

She forced a smile. "You know perfectly well you couldn't sit still through a serious play; you'd be squirming and fidgeting in ten minutes."

"Can't argue that," he grinned, then leaned and kissed her. "Have a nice time, hon, and don't worry about rushing back."

"Thank you, Paul," she answered and felt a knot of tension growing already. "We'll probably stop somewhere after the program and have dinner or something, so don't wait up."

He opened the door for her. "Say hello to Kim," he called after her.

She waved her arm from the car and got in anxious for them to drive off, which Kim did with a roaring jolt. "Hello, darling," Carrie said after needlessly waiting till they were around the corner.

"Hi, there," Kim said with an evil smile. "Long time no see." She pulled up at a dark spot of the road and quickly kissed Carrie on the lips, careful not to smear either of their lipsticks.

"You're crazy!" Carrie said with unconcealed surprise and pleasure. "Don't you know we could get arrested? That somebody might see us?"

"Women're always kissing each other . . . they'd have to catch us necking or fucking and we aren't doing either —worse luck."

"We still could . . ." Carrie said hopefully.

"Not on your life! I'd never get you into town again but there's no problem with getting you into the hay."

"I don't think I approve of your attitude," Carrie said with a smile.

"Oops! Paul's home again. How is the old boy? Still spreading the gospel?"

"I really wish you wouldn't be so hard on him, Kim. I don't go around poking fun at George. . . ."

"Go ahead and poke, who cares about George? Westside Highway or East?"

"East, if you don't care . . . I like going by the river and Sutton Place."

"I don't care. Where does Louise live?"

"Just off Central Park West on Seventy-third Street."

"Money?" Kim asked casually.

"No. Rent-controlled. She's fixed it up nicely and it has a small garden in back. She has a small art gallery midtown, but it hasn't made her rich. I've never met her girlfriend that I recall—they've only been together a little more than a year. You'll probably not be too impressed by Louise at first; she's sort of the quiet type. . . ." Carrie didn't know why she should have to apologize for Louise, who was a perfectly charming woman in her forties. But Kim was so terribly vital and spirited that Carrie worried Louise might be too tame, too sedate, for Kim. Sometimes she really didn't know what Kim saw even in her; there was their age difference, of course, but Carrie certainly wasn't a live wire by any stretch of the imagination. Or perhaps that was precisely what did attract Kim, that Kim could be the young star, no strong competition for the limelight. She didn't know, but she doubted that it mattered as long as Kim loved her. She wanted very much to just hold Kim in her arms and forget about everything else, to feel her young warm body against her own, to stroke her. Besides, she still wasn't very sure of how wise it was to be looking up Louise again after so many years. It would probably just make things more difficult for her since she wouldn't be able to keep up a social friendship with Louise; her life wasn't entirely her own anymore. Impulsively she reached over and took Kim's right hand from the wheel and held it.

"I need that to drive with," Kim said after a moment, her tone a little short but she smiled at the same time.

"What's new in your neighborhood," Carrie asked lightly trying to cover up that she felt slighted, put off.

"Couple next door are getting a divorce, her third, his

first. New family across the street with dreadful furniture, dime-store taste . . . they're all very dark, probably Puerto Ricans for all I know. . . ."

"Well, that should liven up the area," Carrie said.

"Hell, I don't want a bunch of Puerto Ricans running around my house!"

"I doubt that a family makes a bunch. Really Kim, you really amaze me sometimes. In the first place you don't know for sure that they are Puerto Ricans and secondly, what do you know about them anyhow?"

"All I need to know," Kim snorted. "You see how they live in Manhattan; they're dirty and lazy and always smell of rum and garlic. . . ."

"That's the most idiotic thing I've ever heard in my life!" Carried sputtered from genuine shock. "What kind of fanatic prejudice have you been exposed to?"

"Look, Carrie, Christian charity has its place and in theory I agree that everyone has a right to live . . . but not next door to me. Show me a rich Italian, a rich Jew, a rich Puerto Rican, and I'll probably like him provided he comes from a good home and had a good education. Otherwise, let's be honest. Lower classes are lower classes."

"Let's change the subject, Kim," Carrie said coldly. "I don't want to get into an argument about it. Maybe some other time when we're not going out to meet other people."

Kim laughed. "Trouble with you, Carrie Anderson, is you let everything upset you, act as if you're responsible for the whole world. People don't care what happens to you, so why should you care?"

"I'd really prefer not to discuss it now. . . ."

"Okay. Shall I put on the radio while you cool off? See if you can find some jazz, man, like something that moves."

They pulled up at the toll booth at the Triboro and Kim paid the attendant making a little joke about cops getting cuter all the time, and within minutes they were on FDR Drive. Carrie tried very hard to find some justification for Kim's attitude but was hard-put to find any. It was pure and simple bigotry—if such a thing could exist, she thought.

126

She'd have to enlighten Kim somehow, not from any Christian endeavor but just for humanity's sake. After all, she reasoned, anyone living the life of a lesbian certainly has no right to cast any stones!

"Take the 72nd Street turnoff," she said finally, breaking the silence.

"Okay. And, I'm sorry about what I said a minute ago, Carrie. I didn't really mean it. Guess I was just worried about what George would think. . . ."

"I thought you didn't care what George thought," Carrie said with a mixture of resentment and triumph.

"He pays the rent, sweetie, and keeps me in clothes. Gift horses, and hands that feed you and all that."

Carrie had to laugh. "You really lead me a merry chase, do you know that?"

Kim smiled. "Are we parking or just picking them up," she asked as they crossed Lexington Avenue.

"Ring once if we found a parking place, otherwise ring twice and they'll just come out. It's really a little too early to hit the clubs so Louise suggested we come in for a drink or two first."

"Suits me," Kim said and artfully dodged a cab making a U-turn.

"Kim," Carrie said slowly unaware that it had been bothering her before, "do you really love me?"

"Just like a woman!" Kim smiled. "Of course I really love you."

Carrie leaned her head back and let the citified smell of Central Park nature enter her nostrils. "Because, well, I love you very much . . . too much, probably."

"And I love it."

There it was, the "it" again. Carrie wished to God she could be more certain of Kim's feelings, but she was such a strange girl—so quick to laugh and make sarcastic remarks and so impossible to know or be really close to. It was like trying to catch a fish with your hands, always there and always so elusive. She had so much at stake with this girl and had so little security from her. But, she thought, it is her first affair of this kind and so often that produces embarrassment instead of trust. Yet, she found it difficult to ever imagine Kim being embarrassed. ...

Chapter XI

It was a terrible shock to see Louise; she looked terrible. When Carrie had last seen her it was to explain why she was breaking off their friendship—which was, of course, due to her marriage to Paul. Louise had been then an attractive and carefully dressed woman of thirty-seven, careful about her weight and dutiful about daily exercise to keep in shape. But now, eleven years later, it was as if she had completely let herself go, only it was plain that she really hadn't. It was difficult for Carrie to pinpoint exactly what the difference was. Louise was older, naturally, but many women were older still and looked better. No, it was more in the pallid yellow of her skin and the unexpected dark circles under her eyes, the set of her lips which had never been particularly full but now looked like a hard, compressed line. She still had a very presentable figure but Carrie could tell that now she needed the help of a girdle and a heavy-duty bra to keep the illusion. She looked terribly tired, like a lifelong hangover had suddenly caught up with her and her brown eyes were not as bright as they had been, not as lively. It was almost painful for Carrie to look at her and especially at her current girlfriend. Louise had always had the reputation of being able to find and conquer the prettiest gay girls in town; attractive women were drawn to her tall, proud and intelligent manner. It was a running joke in their old crowd that Louise Markham was able—whether she followed through or not—to have any woman walking. But this new girl, this Patricia Loomis, well, she was just *ordinary!* Nice enough, Carrie supposed on such short notice, but not at all the sort of girl Louise would've picked before; but then, the way Louise looked now she probably didn't have the "pick" she used to have. She wondered if Louise supported Patricia as so often "older" women had to do. Carrie sat forward in the basket rocking chair and carefully placed her drink on the mosaic coffee table next to the divan. "Are you in the same kind of business?" she asked Patricia with a polite, inquisitive smile.

"Oh no," Patricia answered with a touch of whining in her voice. "I work in an insurance office, in the audit department."

"That must be interesting," Carrie said hopefully.

"I suppose so; I've never done any other kind of work. Except once, out of high school, I worked in a grocery store for a while. But then I got this job and I've been there ever since, let's see, that's how many years? Well, anyway, it's a lot more than I want to admit!" She giggled girlishly.

My God! Carrie thought, she's one step away from being a moron! She didn't dare look at Kim for fear Kim would be laughing, and less at Louise who was probably suffering agonies strapped with this lump of flesh. "Well, Louise," she said after a heavy silence, "suppose we could be on our way? Kim's been dying to see a lesbian club, about broke my arm to take her."

"Sure, sure, baby." Louise lit a cigarette and offered one to Kim, then to Carrie. "Pat doll, you go put on your coat and let's go."

"I don't want to wear a coat."

"You go put on your coat!" Louise commanded without any attempt to conceal her irritation at being contradicted.

"Oh, all right," Patricia said, getting up and crossing over to the small bedroom off the living room.

Carrie wished violently that they'd not come there tonight, that she'd never seen Louise again much less have to see her like this. She had become terribly dykish, and this thing of calling everyone *doll* or *baby* was really too much. They all gathered at the front door while Patricia looked for her own set of keys.

"You just never know when Lou is going to find some silly young girl and stay out until all hours," Patricia said, giggled, and looked coyly at Louise.

"C'mon, doll, they don't want to hear the story of your life!"

Carrie followed Kim out the door into the long narrow hall leading to the street, with Louise and Patricia trailing. She wondered what Kim was thinking and hoped for the best. Kim had been, for her, strangely silent and seemed to scrutinize everything around her, listened intently to any small exchange of conversation as if lesbians should have a special language of their own.

"One nice thing about living here," Louise called out in a stage whisper, "is the whole building's queer and there're quite a few small clubs in the neighborhood so you don't have to spend all that money on cabs."

"That must be nice," Carrie called back trying to sound impressed if not enthusiastic. But in a way it made sense that they should want to live somewhere where they didn't have to worry what their neighbors would think if they had a boisterous gay party, or a loud argument. She used to get such strange, dark glances from her own neighbors after something like that when she had lived in town; except that she never gave parties in her small apartment, all anybody could've heard was arguments and more arguments. How can two women supposedly living as roommates explain to neighbors statements like "You don't love me anymore!" or, "I saw the way you were looking at her!" It was with great relief that Carrie reached the front door and the street. She didn't think she could move back to Manhattan now for anything; it was so crowded, so suffocating; the air was always heavy with ten million people all breathing in it, cooking in it, driving cars and buses and subways. "Shall we walk it, or take the car?" Carrie asked as they all gathered again outside.

"You kids drive in?" Louise asked putting an arm around Patricia's shoulder.

Carrie wished she wouldn't do that but didn't dare say anything. "We didn't want to have to wait for the New Haven, that's for sure," she said hoping her laugh didn't sound too false.

"Let's walk it, dolls. It's only down the street on 72nd,

just off Columbus . . . won't have any parking problems then."

"All right with you Kim?" Carrie asked.

She shrugged. "Sure, couldn't care less."

"Like your friend, Carrie, doesn't say much."

Carrie smiled. "Never knew her to be shy before, but she'll loosen up with a few drinks." She hated herself even as she said the words. It was so typical of her former self, the "boys talking about their dolls." She felt out of place with Louise and Patricia, a little sorry for them and in turn pompous. Also, that they were so very dressed compared to the skirts and blouses and low heels the other two women wore.

"Can't get over how great you look, Carrie," Louise said as they turned the corner on Central Park West. "Better walk down this street, lots of muggings on Columbus recently."

"I thought the Park was supposed to be worse," Carrie commented and ignored Louise's compliment; she couldn't return it so it was better to say nothing. They walked in two pairs, Kim and Patricia ahead with Patricia talking constantly. Well, Carrie thought, at least Kim won't be forced to try to make conversation.

"Pretty neat looking doll, your Kim," Louise said after a few silent minutes. "Been together long?"

Carrie wasn't too sure how she should answer. "Well, yes and no. I mean, we've known each other for several months but we weren't lovers until very recently. We're . . . we're both still married, you know."

"Kim's married too? Jeez, what rotten luck. What are you going to do with the kids, put them in school or something?"

"It's a little soon to even think of anything like that," Carrie said. "I don't think I could stand to put them in school and not have them around."

"Well, I had a couple of friends once where one had a kid and they about went nuts . . . how do you go around explaining to kids that you've got a double bed, and that you don't date . . . they catch on pretty fast, y'know."

"We've time to think about these things, Louise. Neither of us is in a rush to get a divorce until we know each other better." Carrie amazed herself with what she'd just said. She'd not once really thought of divorce since the affair had begun; but now, with the problems of having husbands around, and what to do with Sambo and Sara, and, well, a *divorce!* She didn't want to think about such a thing, or worse, about what she would have to say to Paul: *I'm sorry, Paul, but I've found another woman and I'm divorcing you.* How could she ever explain such a thing to the children, they loved and needed their father.

"Here we are," Patricia called and stood under a blue awning with raised white letters announcing its name as "The Gay Spot." Carrie wondered how they'd ever had the nerve to name it that, but docilely followed the other three women into the dark, long club. The bar came first, and a huge air-conditioning unit almost obstructed entrance to the back room where tiny round tables gave the wooden floor a polka dot look. The juke box wailed an old romantic Frank Sinatra number, ended abruptly, then began with Nina Simone at peak volume. Surrounding the bar like ants on a carcass were women of every description and a few drag queens in tight chino pants and full face make-up, doing their best to charm the tired bartender. No woman had ever displayed such limp wrists, Carrie thought, and tried to envision herself cooking a dinner with her hands in that position. Booming, tough, female voices could be heard over the juke box demanding two beers, or where's the head? A number of people turned and stared rudely at them as they walked by, but most of the glances were lecherous appraisals of Kim and Carrie in their very feminine dresses.

"There's a spot, c'mon," Louise said loudly and nearly trampled a young, thin girl in slacks.

"Easy there, bud," the girl cautioned Louise and for an awful moment Carrie was terrified there would be one of those ugly fist-fights and hair-pullings the dykes so enjoyed. But Louise had turned about ferociously, then broken into a wide grin. "Hiya, Tiger, didn't see you down there."

"I'll be goddamned," the Tiger muttered and poked a fist into Louise's arm. "Say, just the person I'm looking for. Spare a fin until payday?"

Louise squinted at her. "For boozin' or subway tokens? You still owe me five."

"C'mon, c'mon. I'm good for it, you know that."

"Too bad you're not fem; we could take it out in trade!" They both laughed uproariously and looked to Carrie to share their joke. She managed a smile, but not easily. "Meet a friend of mine from way back," Louise said generously and introduced them. "Been straight for more'n ten years but back in the fold now."

"Say, that's swell," Tiger said. "Welcome back. About that fin. . . ."

"Okay, okay," Louise said like a big brother helping out the kid.

"Nice meetin' you," Tiger said then waved the bill in goodby to them and headed for a bored looking young brunette at the bar.

Louise put her hand under Carrie's elbow and escorted her to the small table where the other two women waited, Patricia still in an unending monologue. Carrie tried to squeeze in next to Kim for whatever consolation she might offer. She dreaded to think what was going on in Kim's mind at that moment. For her own part, she was still trying to digest the Tiger's "Welcome back"—back to what? Could anyone really believe it was better to be gay? She put her hand on Kim's and rested it there. "Too awful?" she asked in a whisper.

Kim looked at her with a strange, masked expression in her eyes. "Just one thing," she whispered back.

"What? . . ."

"Are they kidding?"

Carrie smiled slowly. "No."

Kim shook her head and laughed. "I tell you this is the best blast I've ever seen in my entire life! What a gas!"

"What'll you two have?" Louise asked loudly, "I'll get a waiter over here."

"Beer's fine by me," Carrie said and Kim's nod made it two.

Louise caught a waspish waiter's eye and held up four fingers to him. "I wanted a gin fizz," Patricia whined.

"You're getting beer!"

"They have an adorable floor show here," Patricia informed them quite unperturbed about her gin fizz. "The boys dress up in drag and they're so cute with their dresses 'n things. They put on records and sing—well, not really sing—pretend to be someone singing like whoever's singing on the record, y'know what I mean? . . . Lena Horne or anyone else that's on the record."

"What time does that start," Kim said suddenly interested.

Louise squinted at the large man's watch on her wrist. "Any time now . . . but Pat's right. These fags are a riot."

"You can't very well look down your nose at the gay boys, can you Louise?" Carrie said with a candid smile.

"Sure, why not. The fags don't like us much either," she laughed.

"Oh, Lou, you're just *terrible*. You say the *awfulest* things." Patricia tittered and thumped her elbows heavily on the small table surface. "You and Lou been friends a long time?"

"Must of told you fifteen times, doll baby, we're very old friends," Louise said and gave Patricia a kiss on her cheek.

"Don't," Patricia whined and waved her hand in front of Louise's face.

Suddenly the entire room darkened and a loudspeaker voiced a call for silence and attention. "And now ladies and gentlemen, whichever one you are tonight"—laughter from everywhere—"our usual Saturday night floor show is about to begin. Straighten your falsies, boys, and you girls make sure your jockstraps are on tight 'cause we've got some real surprises for you"—general aplause—"and first off, "The Gay Spot" introduces her own favorite, the last of the red-hot papas, Sophie Fucker. . . ."

A spotlight hit the center of the raised platform in the rear of the club which was now occupied with an eye-defying duplicate of Sophie Tucker. The record scratched for a moment and then the performer mouthed the words with gestures. Everyone applauded the costume and mimicry at the end and Kim touched Carrie on the shoulder. "What was it?"

"A man," Carrie answered, "look for the Adam's apple."

The announcer's voice, followed by three "girls" in Rockette costumes pretending to be the Andrew Sisters cut off further conversation. Carrie wondered how long she'd have to endure the whole thing and glanced over at Kim to see how she was taking all this. Kim was evidently enjoying herself immensely, laughing and exchanging very open flirtatious glances with Louise.

*   *   *   *

Kim asked Carrie to drive them back after they said goodby to the other two girls at their door and climbed into the car. "I'm not tight," she said sleepily, "I'm just tired . . . haven't laughed that much in ages." She curled up on the other side of the seat and rested her head on Carrie's lap.

"You'll get your head crushed like that," Carrie said softly.

"No I won't," she muttered. "George always lets me. . . ."

Carrie started up the car and after a few blocks of adjusting to the larger, more powerful car, turned the radio on softly to keep her company on the way home. She liked having Kim asleep like that, trusting her to get them home safely and take care of her. She could've lived without Kim's admission of identical intimacy with George, but it didn't bother her that much. Carrie's thoughts were too full of the evening, the reencounter with Louise, Patricia and the floor show, even the Tiger's "Welcome back," She supposed that if somehow she were suddenly transplanted to another world her feelings might be the same. And they weren't very optimistic. She wondered if it was simply that she was older, or if it was just the years of quiet straight living that had changed her outlook so. Surely, even if

Louise had changed, she had known other women who'd been even worse and it hadn't bothered her then that she could recall. Was this, then, the fate to which she, too, must come? She had to smile to herself since she doubted that Shakespeare had known any lesbians, but then you never know, maybe he had; certainly it wasn't anything new in the world. There was a kind of desperation about Louise's change, though; a wallowing and satisfaction in switching, or stooping, from the clean-cut and strong character to the well-washed and domineering butch. Yet she had known some lesbians, a very few, who were able to lead the life without letting it become their sum-total reason for living, who remained women different only in their love object without losing their femininity. But the mere admission of how few there were plainly made it the exception rather than the rule. Undoubtedly there was a reason but she didn't wish to dwell on it; what good would it do her to know why Louise, or any of the others gave up? It had happened and there was nothing she could do to help.

Kim stirred only once all the way home, just long enough to ask where they were and kiss Carrie's thigh, then go back to sleep. It had sent a frantic tingling through Carrie's body and she wanted desperately to pull over and park, to wake Kim and kiss her soft lips and take in the perfume of Kim's young body. But it was out of the question; lesbians couldn't do that sort of thing! And now she had to face going home to Paul—to the darkened house, she hoped—and the routine of tomorrow and the next day and the day after that, lying to Paul, dreading his occasional lovemaking, thinking of Kim constantly and wanting to be near her, usually followed by overwhelming tenderness toward the children and guilt. They were going to have to do something, find some solution to all this. She wasn't made of stone, and continuing this deceit, this double life, was making a nervous wreck out of her even if it didn't seem to bother Kim at all. One nice thing about youth, Carrie thought, is that they never think they'll be found out. . . . But it was more than that, she knew. She had come to the very firm conclusion that if she could spend more time with Kim, if they could have long periods together without fear of husbands and children, that she could help Kim to be more loving, more affectionate and dependent upon her even as Carrie was upon Kim. How long could she go on telling herself it was just Kim's youth that prevented a more mutual relationship between them? It was simply an intolerable situation and they had to think of something.

Wearily, Carrie pulled up in front of her own home and turned off the car lights, but left the engine running. "Kim . . . Kim darling . . . wake up now." She stroked the girl's hair and let her fingers rest on the smooth, warm flesh of Kim's cheek.

"Am I home now?" Kim asked sleepily.

Carrie flinched emotionally. The eternal "I", not are "we" or "you", but am "I" home . . . and that there could even be a "home" when they weren't together hurt Carrie deeply. "No, we're at *my* home," she said harshly.

Kim sat up, stretched, and yawned. "Oh. You mad about something?"

Carrie sighed and knew it would be pointless to discuss her feelings at that point. She'd have to wait until some other time when Kim would be more receptive, perhaps after making love when Kim was almost always like a young child needing comfort and protection. "No, I'm not mad at anything . . . just a little tired after all those beers." She opened the car door and slid out letting Kim take the wheel.

"I thought you were mad 'cause I was flirting with Louise," Kim said and yawned again.

Carrie had to smile. She rarely objected to flirting, only to following through. "I doubt that Louise is your type," she answered softly, since sounds at night always carried farther. "Good night, Kim."

"Shall I call you tomorrow, or are you coming over?" Kim put the car lights back on.

"I'm working tomorrow."

"It's Sunday!"

"Can't help that," Carrie answered evenly. Sara's flu

had knocked two days out of her interviewing and she had to have it all completed by Monday.

"Jesus! We never get to fuck anymore," Kim pouted.

"Wouldn't George be home anyway?"

"I could send him off to play tennis or something."

"Well, as you know, much as I'd love to it would be a bit awkward leaving Paul and the kids alone on a Sunday anyway, just to go to your house, I mean."

"Never mind," Kim said coldly, "I'll let George do it!"

Carrie was too angry to say anything, too startled to even attempt to explain her situation. By the time she'd regained her wits Kim had driven off and was turning the corner, leaving only dull red tail lights as a good night. That settles it, Carrie swore silently walking to her door, we'll have to do *something.* . . .

Chapter XII

Monday morning, after everyone had gone, Carrie considered her position. She had had no communication whatsoever with Kim that Sunday and in a strange sort of way it was a relief. Most of that morning and part of the afternoon had gone to interviewing, then she returned home and started their traditional Sunday dinner of stuffed chicken—she'd been careful to explain to Paul that working that day was the first time, and that it would probably never happen again that she'd be forced to leave them on the weekend. But at least she'd not been under the usual pressure of hoping there was a chance to see Kim somehow, to talk to her, so that she was a good deal more relaxed than she'd been in quite some time. It was strange about love—even straight love, she supposed, going by literature and passion murders—that finding someone you could be sure of, someone whom you knew without question loved you just as much, just as intensely, was next to impossible to find. It seemed that the only times you could be really confident was when you couldn't return the love, like between herself and Paul, she thought. But that wasn't accurate either, she had to admit. They loved and respected each other, but there was none of the consuming passion, the fierce energy and anguish which Carrie felt for Kim. Even if she had a vocabulary larger than the Oxford Dictionary she knew she'd never be able to articulate how she felt about Kim, nor had for that matter, about Beth, her first love. There was a great similarity in her feelings toward both women, different as they were from one another. The same complicated tearing inside herself, the fears and insecurities, the vexing and hidden desire to be constantly reassured, told that Kim loved her, the spasmodic aching to have Kim hold her and comfort her. If she could only be more certain of Kim, if she only had the time to be with her and get accustomed to her love so that it didn't eat at her like carrions picking on the open wound of a still-alive but helpless animal. Oh, novelists sometimes wrote about the anguish of love, but it never encompassed its complete, pernicious range. The closest she could recall was in the book *Of Human Bondage;* that doctor or whatever he was and the street-girl. Carrie had well understood his feelings, his fear, loathing, and compulsion to have that harlot . . . Hadn't Bette Davis played the part? She couldn't remember; it was the book which had impressed her. Yet his had been a kind of masochistic compulsion. He knew that his love was not returned, yet persisted. Carrie believed her emotions infinitely less endurable simply because she didn't know, couldn't know. She wanted to believe in the love, but couldn't be sure; Kim said she loved her, and on a few rare occasions would even be demonstrative of it, but it was like living on rations, constantly hoping for a little more proof, something more tangible, something which was always withheld. Did Kim, too, look up from whatever she was doing and have a pleasure-pain longing to touch Carrie, to feel her and be comforted in a blanket of understanding, tenderness, and passion? Carrie did, and at times she could and nearly did cry just to see Kim, the way sunlight would catch her face and throw shadows, an expression, a smile, a repose . . . moments that reinforced Kim's image and existence, separated Kim from any other living person and stirred a dark cave of nebulous, fluctuating emotions within Carrie.

She didn't know, she just didn't know what Kim thought or felt and it sometimes made her so frantic she wished she could shake the words, the truth, out of Kim and put her soul at ease. The few times Kim had said she loved her was in answer to Carrie's questioning, or after love-making; but it never had the tone of soft earnestness Carrie so needed; nor did her eyes ever show the warmth of unexpected yet quieting tenderness which would sustain Carrie and obliterate any doubts. Carrie had sometimes, of late, wished that she were a hypnotist, or possessed a truth potion to extort the truth from Kim and know it once and for all; either erase her torment or be compelled to confront the shattering opinion Kim might hold for her. Yet this was quite out of the question, she knew, and the only other possible solution was to have Kim to herself, alone and uninterrupted, without fear for as long as she could until Kim should confide her feelings to her. How selfish and cruel lovers are, she thought, to withhold their inner emotions, to dangle their love, doling it out in so many grams per meeting instead of opening themselves, sharing their hearts regardless of what hurt might come later. Carrie coldly feared being hurt but knew that she far preferred the hurt of giving to the hurt of being deprived; she knew no other way to love but to give openly of herself, to spread her thoughts before Kim like a book so that Kim should always understand her and be sure of her; but Kim was apparently the reverse, holding her love in abeyance like a daytime serial. If Kim loves me, Carrie decided, I must break through somehow, I must make her understand that she's torturing me needlessly. . . .

Carrie sighed and forced herself to clean up the breakfast dishes before calling Kim. She wanted time to organize her thoughts but she knew that there was really nothing to organize. Her conscious mind was a camouflage of

140

many-colored pebbles blocking the way of the tumultuous cavern of subconscious knowledge and decisions, already formulated, pushing and thrusting to get past the barrier, to burst out and be recognized, sun themselves in wakeful awareness and action. And it was with trepidation and, at the same time, ruthless determination that she finally dialed Kim's number.

"N-E-2 . . ." she whispered to herself as she dialed and waited for Kim to answer.

"Hello!" Kim's voice came like a curse through the receiver.

Carrie kept her voice even and light. "Good morning, Mrs. Willis. This is your New Rochelle Welcome Committee. . . ."

"Well, N.R.W.C., can you fix the plumbing?"

Carrie grinned. "Personal service guaranteed."

"Godamn john's stopped up . . . must be George throwing his cigar butts in it again. God I hate this house!" Kim paused. "What's on your mind?"

"Mostly wanted to hear your voice," Carrie said, "but there's something I wanted to talk to you about anyhow. Mind if I come over?"

There was a short silence. "Well, frankly, Carrie, I . . . ah . . . I have an appointment for lunch . . . it would be cramming things a bit."

Carrie wouldn't have taken any particular notice of Kim's being busy except for the way she was stalling around about it. "Well, it wasn't anything terribly urgent," she said spitefully. "I just thought we might take a moment or two to discuss our situation . . . where we stand with each other."

"What's to discuss?" Kim said in a tight voice. "It's perfect the way it is, isn't it? We've both got security and kicks . . . what else do you want?"

Carrie bit her lower lip trying to keep the painful tears away, to keep control of herself. Kim had such a magnificent way of completely pulling the rug out from under her, of making her feel the way she had when Martha, her high school crush, had dumped her. Not that Kim said anything about dumping, but, well, it was in her lack of concern, her refusal to see anyone else's needs but her own. Granted, Kim certainly had been much more giving these past few weeks, much warmer toward Carrie; but what else could she be toward a lover? Where did real, honest emotion end and badly-concealed toleration begin? The worst part was that if Carrie dared to say anything to Kim about it, to talk of love instead of kicks, Kim would not really understand. She would, of course, retract and reword, but Carrie couldn't genuinely depend on Kim's sincerity—she could not really depend on Kim. It grated her and tortured her, but to say anything would only make matters worse.

Finally, Carrie forced herself to make some kind of response to Kim's question. "I suppose it's not so much what I want, but what I'm not getting."

"And what's that mean?" Kim said.

Carrie stifled a sigh of frustration. "Nothing, Kim. I don't know why this got to be such a big thing. I thought I'd come by and you're busy, so I won't."

"Then why do you sound so angry?" Kim asked warily.

"I'm not angry. There were a few things on my mind which I'd have liked to discuss with you as soon as possible. Not because of any urgency or time limit, but just because I love you and would like to share my thoughts, hopes and fears with you. I know it sounds ridiculous to you, Kim, but some people might have offered to break their luncheon appointment in order to be a companion as well as a sex-partner."

"Oh for crissakes! You're not my husband, Carrie. What's been fun is that we're not tied to each other, constantly having to account for every minute. I'd break the goddamn appointment except that I can't. They're . . . they're coming into Westchester from the city . . . for all I know they're already on the train. What could I say to them anyhow—"Sorry, but my lesbian girlfriend and I have to discuss our relationship?" Be reasonable, Carrie!"

"I'm trying to be."

"Then don't put the screws on me. You start acting like

an abandoned five-year old and we *will* have something to talk about!"

"Is that a threat?"

"Oh, for God's sake . . .forget it! I'll talk to you later when you can be more adult about the whole thing."

Carrie was aware of a crawling fury when she realized Kim had hung up on her. She slammed her own receiver down and returned to the sink, staring out the window as if her own wrath would level everything in her line of vision. She turned and left the kitchen, then slowly walked upstairs to dress; might as well go into town and run a few errands. Maybe she'd go into Bloomingdale's and browse for awhile, or stop in at the Pottery Shop and talk to Frances—anything but sit around and sulk. It was an impossible situation, she knew. Something was going to have to give, and quite soon, but Kim wasn't making it any easier.

Just before noon she drove the Volkswagen up to the parking lot behind Bloomingdale's and walked around the store instead of using the rear entrance. It was a dismal day, heavy with rain clouds, and with a humid chill in the air. She walked up Main Street toward North Avenue in an ambling, disinterested way until she was across the street from Arnold Constable's, then turned around and stood in a nearly helpless, bewildered way. The traffic on North Avenue was light for that hour of the day. She remained motionless on the corner watching the cars until she spotted a Ford convertible coming from the direction of the station, a car the same color as Kim's—she'd never seen another like it in New Rochelle. As it approached the intersection the signal changed, and Carrie realized that it was indeed Kim driving it, her directional lights indicating she was going to turn up Main Street and head toward Larchmont. She wasn't alone, but it took a few seconds for the identity of the passenger to register in Carrie's mind, and a few seconds longer to believe her eyes. It was Louise!

Carrie groaned and felt the tears smart her eyes. It was simply too much for one day. Everything about the past month was catching up with her, overpowering her.

The discovery about Paul, her guilt about her past and failure as his wife, and her weakness with Kim. None of it made any sense, no sense at all! She wheeled around and nearly ran down the street and back to the car. Driving the short distance in record speed, she screeched into her driveway and let herself into the house as if demons were chasing her. She felt as if gremlins were squeezing her intestines through a sieve. There was no evidence to make her believe that Kim and Louise were having an affair . . . but nor was there any to the contrary. If Kim had to refer to Louise as "they," then something was not quite right. For that matter, Louise was supposed to be Carrie's friend—why hadn't Kim invited her along if everything was on the up-and-up. Maybe the two of them hadn't done anything yet . . . but it was coming up and no doubt about it. Carrie walked around the house too stunned to have any real reaction—unable to muster anger or hate. She just couldn't understand what was motivating Kim. Now, more than ever, Carrie wanted to prove to herself that Kim was not just a selfish child out for kicks, but a confused personality unable to recognize honest love when she got it; it was vitally important to believe that, otherwise . . . Otherwise—what? The thought that she might love, but not be loved in return, was one Carrie could cope with; but that she should love and have it used, abused, laughed at, was more than she could stand. It couldn't be true. It simply could not.

She was positive that Kim needed a strong, unwavering love to believe in; that with that kind of love she would learn to relax, to be able to give of herself. The mere fact that Kim was being so stupid about meeting Louise nearly convinced Carrie of that. To have Louise come to New Rochelle where it was so immediately likely that Carrie would see them was just begging to be caught, to be punished, to hurt Carrie in order to command attention. That's what the analysts would probably call it, Carrie reasoned, an attention-getting device. It had to be that. Oh, certainly Kim was curious and on the wild side, and she'd lose no opportunity to engage in some new adventure; but that was part of her insecurity which Carrie was sure she could overcome. If she only had the time to be alone with Kim . . . if she could only be with her all the time!

Carrie stretched out on the living room couch and tried to think—but all her thoughts seemed to lead to a dead end. She could do nothing unless she and Kim were together. . . .

*   *   *   *

It had been a tortuous afternoon and evening. Carrie had gone through the hours mechanically. Her mind had stumbled into a rut based on a solution only being achieved through constant devotion and proof of her love for Kim. She was so involved in her thoughts that she'd not even noticed Paul's beginning irritation with her moods, his remarks that it was time she shaped up. Kim had not called her back that afternoon and this, too, left Carrie immune to everything outside her own emotions. She realized that she had probably rushed Kim yesterday, made her defensive, which was not the way to handle Kim. She would have to be more careful, more patient.

Carrie once again got the family off in the morning and was about to call Kim, to apologize, to pretend she knew nothing about Kim's meeting with Louise, to do anything to bring Kim to her senses. But instead her own phone rang and wishing to rid herself of whomever was calling as quickly as possible, she snatched the receiver and brusquely said hello.

"Hi, it's me," Kim's voice announced.

"Kim? Oh, Kim, I'm so glad you called . . . I was just about to call you."

Kim laughed lightly. "You sound as if you thought I'd died, or something. Anyhow, I thought if you still wanted to have that talk that you might want to come over now. Just remember that I'm not too bright in the morning," she said.

Carrie felt so relieved that Kim had made the gesture

of her own free will, that it was like getting a stay of execution. She didn't care now if they ever "talked" as long as they could be together, have their moments of happiness. Finally she managed to answer. "Great . . . but I've got to get dressed yet . . . I'll just throw on a pair of slacks. . . ."

"Okay. When you get here, you get here. No rush. I'm not dressed either."

They said goodbye and Carrie went upstairs to change. As she got ready she practiced different approaches to all the things she wanted to say, all that was in her heart and mind. She had to be careful not to be so vehement that she would frighten Kim away with her intensity. She considered being casual, serious, loving, aloof—every manner she could conceive of. It wasn't until she was putting on her make-up that the extent of her nervousness and upset really sunk in; until she had the tube of red-orange lipstick in her fingers and held it trembling before her lips in front of the mirror. Her hands had only shaken like that once before in her life, and it had been the day Beth and she had had that last argument; that final decisive unspoken agreement that their affair was over and dead.

Half an hour later Carrie walked into Kim's house, her body swirling with so many emotions that she couldn't possibly separate one from the other. She was filled with adoration, compassion, horror, panic, dread, desire, fear; every nerve struggled for attention and release. Yet, somehow, she was able to keep some semblance of control.

"Just coffee, thanks," Carrie said as Kim preceded her into the kitchen. She felt oddly aloof saying it, but she was anxious to keep the level of this meeting on a serious but nonemotional ground—at least, on the surface—so that Kim would not withdraw from her. There was a half-empty glass of wine sitting on the kitchen sideboard which Carrie couldn't help but notice. "New kick?" she asked Kim pleasantly pointing to the glass. "Bit early, don't you think."

"Hardly," Kim answered. "The suburban housewife's

answer to Miltown and coffee. Makes the day more bearable. You should try it."

"I'm not too fond of wine in the first place, but the thought of it at ten in the morning would be enough to send me back to bed." Carrie marveled at her own ability to discuss banalities when there was so much she wanted to say and do. She longed to take Kim in her arms and hold her; nothing else, just hold her, feel her warmth and draw strength from her nearness.

Kim shrugged and loudly banged the kettle on the stove, slopping some of the water. "Instant all right?"

"Sure." She took in Kim's bedtime attire of George's pajama top and inanely found herself comparing it to her own preference for sheer nightgowns or shorties; even during her exclusively gay period she had preferred feminine nightwear.

"You smiling at my rig?" Kim asked staring down at her long, strong legs exposed beneath the top.

"A little," Carrie smiled. "I would have expected some Rita Hayworth get-up more."

Kim leaned back against the sink. "I always sleep naked —throw on square George's top in the mornings just to keep my shoulders warm. He has a fit every morning and I ignore him every morning. He likes his pajamas all ironed and fresh looking. Only time he doesn't glower at me's when we've been fucking." She ran her fingers gently over her lips. "Still sore, the bastard."

Carrie tried to ignore the reference to Kim's sex life with George. She didn't want to think about it, even to know about it. "Where's your cook?" she asked changing the subject.

"Told you once she never comes by until after four. You take cream, don't you?"

"We're even," Carrie said trying to smile. "I didn't remember about your cook, and you should certainly know by now how I like my coffee." She wished Kim would give her an opening so they could get to the point.

"Just answer the question, yes or no," Kim said in a

harassed way standing in front of the enormous refrigerator.

"Yes," Carrie answered stiffly as Kim placed the steaming cup of black coffee before her. She took in the room and reaffirmed that she never had liked the kitchen bar-like set up that Kim had; she liked tables and chairs. It felt like a Chock-Full-o'-Nuts stand otherwise, pressuring one to drink up and move on. Kim placed a wax carton quart of milk on the counter and sat down noisily next to Carrie on the bar stool. The pajama top was too short to provide any modesty and fell open exposing Kim's inner thighs and the inviting tuft of blond pubic hairs. Carrie remained superficially indifferent long enough to pour the milk and stir the mixture a second or two. But the naked proximity was more than she could take, especially since it had been so long since they'd lain together, since she'd enjoyed the feel of this gentle-rough hair upon her own thighs, against her. . . . She felt her face and legs grow warm then hot and a shaft of heat seemed to burst into her head from the base of her skull. She leaned forward slightly and placed her hand in between Kim's legs. Kim turned and faced her, an expression almost of shock on her face, and Carrie kissed her eyes, her wonderfully soft cheeks, her lips, hoping that now she could pour out her love, her thoughts.

"Jesus!" Kim swore quietly and pulled away from Carrie's lips. "Take it easy, willya? George about chewed my mouth off last night . . . hurts like hell!"

Like some driven, frightened animal, Carrie drew back and felt her mouth pull into an ugly grimace as she swept all the cups and plates off the counter sending them splashing and breaking onto the floor. "Are you heartless?" she demanded, "a sadist? Don't you know how I feel when you talk about you and George?" She jumped off the stool and stood glaring at Kim like some undetected fungus. "Why don't you tell me exactly what he does, how he teases you first with his penis, how you enjoy going down on him and letting him do you, how it feels when he enters you! Why don't you, Kim. We'll put it on tele-

148

vision on the late late show so the whole world will know, so I can sit at home and play with myself watching him make love to you . . . you'd like that idea, wouldn't you! Or maybe you'd like a quiet little orgy—the three of us, or would it be rude of me to invite Paul too! Poor man doesn't get much from me these days 'cept a dry wiggle or two. Oh, yes! Let's invite Paul by all means!"

"What's gotten into you?" Kim demanded. "You gone nuts?"

"Of course," Carrie laughed. "Nuts. Nuts 'n balls in all the walls," Carrie invented in a sing-song tone.

Kim got down from the bar stool and hesitantly walked over to Carrie standing in the kitchen doorway. She raised her hand tentatively to Carrie's hair and then down to her cheek and stroked it soothingly. "I'm sorry, Carrie . . . I didn't think . . . well, you *know* that George. . . ."

Carrie burst into uncontrollable sobs and pulled Kim to her roughly, held her to her like a child after a long separation, ran her hands down to Kim's buttocks and felt their smooth softness, kneading them, pulling her closer and tighter against herself. "Oh, Kim," she said finally, ashamed of herself and her anger and hoping desperately that Kim would understand, would perhaps now open up to her. "Kim darling, I love you so much . . . can't you understand how I feel? I can't go on living away from you, knowing that George makes love to you, sucks on your breasts where I so much want to be . . ." She almost added Louise's name to her inner terrors, but stopped herself in time.

"Well, sure, Carrie," Kim's voice sounded distant and unsure, "I don't like being away from you either."

"Every hour I think of you, wonder where you are, what you're doing . . . and want to love you, touch you, feel your body, wrap you up inside of me and carry you around always. . . ."

"But we can't, Carrie, you know we can't," Kim said quietly.

"You could leave George," Carrie said almost as one word, the thought spilling out of her like water overrunning

149

a basin, "and I could leave Paul . . . the children would live with us, you'd like that Kim, you said you liked having them around, remember? They don't have to know why, we could be careful about it, time it so that it wasn't obvious, and it would only be natural that we'd live together afterwards, wouldn't it? Wouldn't it?" she demanded fearfully as Kim struggled out of her grasp and stepped back staring at her with unblinking, almost feverish eyes. Carrie's arms fell to her side and she felt crazed and convulsed, beaten and trampled.

"Me live with you? Me leave George for *you!*" Kim spat the questions out and suddenly doubled over with laughter, a taunting cheap gargle shaking her body. "Have you completely lost your mind?"

Carrie could do nothing but watch her. It wasn't so much what Kim had said as how she had said it. If Kim had stretched out her hands and grasped Carrie's throat for the sheer amusement of watching her eyes pop out of her head, her face turn blue and purple gasping for air, her tongue a swollen mass hanging out of her face, if Kim had done this for the plain joy of inflicting pain, it would have hurt Carrie less, far less. But Kim was still laughing, still bouncing Carrie's love like a rubber ball against a spiked wall.

"Look, sweetie, you fuck great but whatever made you think I'd give up my life and comfort to be some miserable dyke housewife like those creep friends of yours. *That's* where *you* belong, sweetie, not me. Always bugging me about whether I love you or not, about drove me buggy with your mooning face and nagging! Go crawl up some other gal's ass if you think I'd give up anything for a lesbian life. You aren't even rich! Your alimony wouldn't even cover my charge accounts much less support those little brats of yours. Sure I liked screwing with you, and hanging around your place was all right for a while, kind of a kick until I got tired of it, and mind you Carrie, I'm grateful to you; I learned just how well-off I am not having any kids. You come waltzing in here like some big man with a big prick and start breaking up dishes and screeching . . . I've got neighbors, y'know, I don't want to get tagged with a lesbian. . . ."

"Shut up!" Carrie screamed. "Shut up shut up shut up!"

"Don't tell me what to do in my own house!" Kim hissed. "For all I know you've got half the housewives in New Rochelle all half-queer . . . go get one of *them* to move in with you. Just fuckin' doesn't make me a pervert like you; I'm no queer and I told you that from the start. . . ."

"Then why did you meet Louise secretly?" Carrie yelled.

Her body felt as if every vein and artery were bursting with hatred and disgust, her fingers flexed uncontrollably, but then she added, "Shut up." She whispered it quietly but with such venom that Kim backed off toward the door again. "Shut up Kim or I swear I'll kill you."

"You *have* gone nuts," Kim barely breathed and backed steadily closer to the doorway.

Carrie made no effort to stop her; except for her hands no part of her moved. The expression on Kim's face was a thrilling reward of its own, the fear and panic, the uncertainty. If anyone had ever told Carrie before that she'd be capable of so much violence she'd have laughed. Kim kept backing up until she was halfway past the dining alcove and had reached the glass doors to the garden, her eyes darting from place to place in the room as if seeking a weapon for defense. Carrie let her reach the doors and then coldly, deliberately trying to frighten Kim, she stepped slowly, purposefully toward her, something very like a smile on her face. Kim only hesitated for a second then in a scramble of arms and legs pushed the doors open, seemed to take inordinately long to get past them, and closed them again peering at Carrie from behind the safety of the glass, poised and ready to run if necessary.

Carrie suddenly felt as if she were playing a part, a role in a play, and she'd given the role everything she had. She was exhausted but triumphant; she had left the audience in a state of emotional immobility, mouths slightly agape, while she herself could now return to the privacy of her dressing room and laugh at the plot as intangible, having nothing to do with real life. And with this knowledge, she did laugh, a strange choking laugh and found herself walking past Kim's window-framed body into the living room and out the front door to her small car. It seemed an exceptionally sunny day, like the feeling she sometimes had when she'd awake from a midday nap with a nightmare; the world always seemed so reassuring, so safely void of nightmares. She made a U-turn and glanced at Kim's house just in time to see the front door slam shut and the curtain of the living room window pulled slightly to one side. Inanely, all Carrie could think was that Kim had now learned better than to hide in people's cars with picnic lunches. . . .

Chapter XIII

It took Carrie a little more than three weeks to be completely herself again, three weeks of concentrated self-examination and contemplation. That she had been a fool? There was no doubt of that. That she had squandered her love, had been grossly stupid in jeopardizing her family was beyond reviewing. All those things were suddenly as self-evident as the most elementary algebraic formulas: Stupidity, no matter how you multiply or divide it equals stupidity. These things no longer were clubs for recriminations to Carrie. What she had learned, and could now even be thankful to Kim for, was that she had wasted eleven years. *Wasted.* She may as well have elected to sleep through them. *None so blind as those who won't see* ceased to be just a hackneyed phrase but now a truth with which to club herself. She'd pined for passion from life, titilating love . . . background music for every kiss! And she hated and swore at herself for her wanton thickness of skull.

She went numbly and automatically through those weeks

lost in her own thoughts except for when the children addressed her, or Paul insisted on her attention. Strangely, all three of them had seemed to sense her need to be alone, her time to reflect, and gave her an enormous berth which she certainly didn't believe she deserved. Even Paul ceased commenting on her irrational behavior and was quiet.

It wasn't thoughts of whether or not she was really gay that wrapped her silently from them, but a long-delayed evaluation of what she had to offer life and what it could offer her. Gay? It would always be there; she accepted that now. Realized how stupid she had been trying to suppress it all those years . . . by the time Kim had entered her life she was no better than a drunken sailor, who'd just hit port after a year at sea—seeking a woman, any woman, who could relieve him. She could read a newspaper, eat an apple, if she wanted to, but until that first relief there could be no other thought. The element of a lasting, solid love could never be present under such circumstances. It took so much understanding to love, so much patience and willingness to share—not just give—and for eleven years *she had had this from Paul* yet blindly, adolescently deprived him of herself, of being his wife, of giving him a home. She'd not once been woman enough to even take the initiative about love-making with him, either by word or action. And she wondered now how he had stood her withdrawal from him, yet knowing of it control himself.

Certainly his love was far deeper than she had ever appreciated before. He was not the one to place everything on a sexual basis, as she thought all this time; *she* was. Instead of accepting sex as a natural part of any marriage, as the physical acceptance of Paul and his love, as a sharing in terms of pleasure their respect for each other, she had frozen this part of herself away damaging not only Paul, but herself as well. Paul could easily have divorced her during the early years of their marriage but he loved her enough to want her as his wife, to need her companionship. And if his natural needs had driven him to other women, was it not proof of his honest love for her? His infidelity was nothing more than a courtesy to her, a desire to eliminate any unpleasantness from their marriage, instead of allowing his needs to become so magnified that more and more arguments would eventually destroy all respect between them. It had not been weakness on his part, but strength. It was she who had placed their whole relationship on sex by its very negative attitude on her part.

She had lived in semi-reality, seeking and dwelling always on the proverbial "butterflies in the stomach." But what was that besides a sexual response? It wasn't respect and devotion, it was simple chemistry. The very thing she had feared was the one thing she had perpetrated! Carrie now knew what she had done to Paul, to their marriage, even as she now realized that the Kims of the world would always deride; they were the poachers of the world, bees squatting temporarily but long enough to take their own poisonous pollen. She had let sex overrule her and couldn't help a certain amount of self-pity at the squandering of her time and emotions.

Even if she was not gay, there would also be times when she would meet some attractive man and think to have an affair. It was natural; it was human. Sexual attraction did not necessarily confine itself to the opposite sex, and even as a normal woman must face and overcome outside attractions ,she too would have to honestly combat her own desires. She did not for a moment think that she would never again be attracted to another woman . . . but now she believed herself mature enough not to give in to it. She would have to grow up, accept herself and control her emotions with understanding rather than fear—as she had the past eleven years—face her gayness like a diabetic faces his strenuous diet. The sum total, Carrie recognized, was worth more than any sex act alone could provide, or any amount of sugar.

Paul had known that all along, and his refusal to give up their marriage solely on the basis of sexual incompatability proved it beyond any doubt. It was Carrie's adolescent attitude toward sex that had nearly ruined their marriage and she hated herself now for having been such an ignorant, self-centered fool. Thrills and tingles belonged in dime-store novels—not in real life. If they happen to come along with the marriage, how fortunate; but after the honeymoon, after the routine set in, how many couples ever continued to have them anyway? She wanted to crawl into a dark hole and hide; yet her awakening made that impossible; her belated recognition of responsibility not only to Paul and her family, but to herself as a person, as a woman.

*   *   *   *

Paul had not in the last few weeks questioned her about her friendship with Kim. She had told him tersely, at the time immediately following her argument with her, that they had had a falling-out and that they had mutually agreed to end the friendship. He'd let it go at that. By the end of the second week she had begun to be more herself, more sure of where she stood and what her life held. Now, in the third week since she had seen Kim, she was more at peace, more vibrant than she had ever felt in her entire life. Carrie had not made Paul into a saint in any way, but she had certainly learned what a hell of a life she had given him and how much she had to learn, and do, to make it up to him—and in so doing, make it up to herself as well. He wasn't a saint, he was a man—and one who loved her. She admired him now as never before; his patience and his ability to avoid what might have been an unbearable marital relationship. Not many men would have done what Paul had. Oddly, this realization had not made her feel more guilty. She supposed she should, but the realization of the depth of his devotion, of how very lucky she was, totally overpowered any other thought. And, too, she recognized how near to a nervous breakdown she had come during her infatuation with Kim, and knew that its escape was due mostly to Paul's strength.

As for Kim, all she could feel was pity; Carrie couldn't

even hate her. Her feelings were dead toward the girl, as if Kim had never existed.

It was on Tuesday, three weeks to the day after Carrie's last moments with Kim, that Paul came home early from the office and suggested they go out to dinner instead of on their usual day. Carrie, with a new excitement, agreed readily. They rode in comfortable silence to the restaurant. Once inside and seated, Carrie automatically ordered a brandy Alexander instead of a martini but didn't notice Paul's slow satisfied smile, until she raised the glass in toast. She knew why he was smiling, what the simple return to old habit signified for them both. Carrie felt the tears building up but forced them back and took his hand across the table and held it firmly. Even a normal gesture such as hand-holding took on a new significance for her; it was normal. She could hold hands with him in public; she could not worry about anything she did because it was natural and acceptable to all onlookers. How much simpler, how more reassuring than a homosexual relationship. I've changed, Carrie thought, long before Kim . . . but it took that relationship to prove it to me. She didn't doubt for a moment that much of her affair had been prompted by her hurt at Paul's infidelity; but what she had not realized at the time was that if she could be so hurt by him that she did love him more than she had been able to admit. The whole affair now seemed to her to be nothing more than an escape from that normal love. She wasn't sure why. Carrie did not know enough about reactions and counter-reactions that the more learned laymen would glibly explain to her; she just marveled at her own blindness and good fortune to have escaped the consequences.

She squeezed Paul's hand more tightly. "Paul?"

"Yes, darling," he answered, his lean face serious and waiting.

"Have I ever told you that I love you very much. . . ."
She knew she hadn't, but it came easily now and she'd never meant anything more in all her life; knew that the

156

words spoken to others before him arose from passion rather than genuine, lasting love.

He grinned slowly. "I thought you did," he said. "That's why I hung around for so long." He paused, and with his free hand lifted his cocktail glass in a second toast. "Welcome back, of course . . . but mostly, well, just plain welcome."

She was surprised by his tone of voice, surprised and even a little amused. He sounded very much as if he had known all along about her affair with Kim, about her entire past perhaps, and couldn't help thinking what a laugh that would be on herself. But she wouldn't ask him, and she knew he'd never mention it. They would probably never think of it again, much less talk about it. It seemed so unnecessary, superfluous. But maybe, one day when they were very old, maybe then she could ask him if he'd known . . . when they were very very old. . . .

ALSO BY
PAULA CHRISTIAN

EDGE OF TWILIGHT
THIS SIDE OF LOVE
LOVE IS WHERE YOU FIND IT
ANOTHER KIND OF LOVE
AMANDA